THE ENGLISH CANTOS

VOLUME 1: HELLWARD

JAMES SALE

First published 2019 © 2019 James Sale

The right of James Sale to be identified as authors of this work has been asserted by them in accordance with sections 77 and 78 of the Copyright, Designs and Patents Act 1988.

ISBN: 979-8-654151919

Printed and bound by Amazon KDP

Cover artwork "I am here and there" by Linda E. Sale. Cover designed by Joseph Sale.

❀ Created with Vellum

For Dr Tom Woodman, scholar, mentor, and friend

CONTENTS

INTRODUCTION

I kicked off writing the English Cantos in October 2017, and now 2 years and 8 months later the first volume of the 3-volume sequence is complete. It's a massive relief; but also a massive challenge as I contemplate how to continue Volume 2 and sustain this level of writing. But before I talk about what's next, what are the English Cantos? What is their purpose and what are they trying to achieve? Also, why am I writing this?

Early on, in my teenage years – about aged 13 – I got hooked on poetry, both reading it and attempting to write it. I became aware, although at first in a very hazy way, that certain poets were speaking to my very soul; that words were magic, and that the poet was a wizard with them; that the poet could conjure up spirits from 'the vasty deep', if indeed they were so moved. And, in that moving, they moved us, entranced us, and we were held under their spell.

At school I successfully completed A levels in Pure Maths, Applied Maths and Physics and was offered a place at university to study Physics. But by this time, the Muse had uncontrollably got possession of me: I had to go further with the study of words and their poetry. This meant a complete turn-round of my projected career. In doing so, I encountered the greats: Homer, Virgil, Dante, Spenser, Shakespeare and Milton. To read them was – to say the least – a real eye-opener!

Milton in particular fascinated me. As Dr Johnson observed (and given that he was no fan of Milton the man, or his political or theological views), 'Whoever soared so high and for so long?' How did Milton do that? I have spent nigh-on 50 years now, brooding on that question, and chasing down potential answers. My favourite answer, that was never completed, is Keats: the two Hyperion fragments only give me a little less pleasure than Milton himself, and certainly if he had written nothing else (which fortunately he did) would have placed him in the first rank of English poets. For the performance is nothing short of astonishing: there is that same elevation of style, that same sublimity of conception that marks Milton's work. True, however, that Keats was not able to sustain it, and the poems do flag in places. But that said, they are a tremendous achievement. If only one compares them with the highly enjoyable, but synthetically heroic, Idylls of the King, by Tennyson, one can see – feel - Keats' superiority. But Keats died at 26, tragically.

However, somebody had attempted epic, why not me?

There are a number aspects of writing epic that I think that I cannot deal with or cover here in a short introduction. For what I want to mention is the technical aspect. But in passing I would mention as of foremost importance, the poet's theology or philosophy or what might be called their world-view; their system, in other words, for interpreting reality. For sublimity, an essential quality of epic, cannot be founded on a simplistic, facile or false ideology. Such epics, based on such weak core beliefs, can only be simple, facile or false in the doctrines and stories they promote.

One reason why Dante's Divine Comedy can be entered into the pantheon of 'greatest epic ever written' is because the belief system behind it is awesome. By which I do not mean that one needs to be a Roman Catholic in that overt sense that Dante was. No, it's the profound belief system behind the overt belief system. In Dante's case, one example of this is the belief in human freewill; that choices matter; that everything we do has some sort of eternal resonance; and then when we face the world, this works itself out at the three levels we encounter in the poem. By predicating such importance to human decision-making ('the drama of the soul's choice'), and elevating it to a point whereby even God cannot reverse the consequences of such decisions, we invest humanity with a grandeur that can only be called sublime. There is the deep pathos of those who are lost; there is the hope of those on the mountain who still might climb; and then there is the almost blinding light of the beatific vision and those who attain it. Quite, quite inspiring in every single way. At least, I think so: today the concept of hell is unpopular to the exact degree that freedom of the will is unpopular; for it would appear that now 'we' all want to be victims instead.

And for seven centuries (Dante celebrates 700 years since his death in 1321) people have known, through the reading and experience of the poem, that this is remarkable and not something that should be lost. Not something either that we should allow simplistic and socialistic philosophies of 'equality' to suppress. (As Dorothy L Sayers perceptively noted: 'We cannot but be sharply struck by the fact that two of our favourite catch-words have absolutely no meaning in Heaven: there is no *equality* and there is no *progress*.') Here is the human spirit in all its glory, including the glory to fail, to not be 'equal', to be of no account in the sight of Almighty God. This is grappling with 'reality' at its most intense, its most personal, and – paradoxically – its most universal.

Conversely, and to be clear, simply having a profound philosophy – theology – ideology will not in itself make a great poem. Indeed, the danger of philosophy generally is a dull discursiveness: an explication that is academic in every sense of the word. I have written elsewhere of the concept of the 'Muse', so will not attempt to deal with her here. However, inspiration is a primary requisite for being a poet. As Socrates observed: 'I soon realised that poets do not compose their poems with real knowledge, but by inborn talent and inspiration, like seers and prophets who also say many things without any understanding of what they say . . .'

But to return to the issue of the technical aspect of writing epic poetry. So far as English poetry and verse goes, we know that meter is essential, for as the influential critic I.A. Richards expressed it: 'Meter for the most difficult and most delicate utterances is the all but inevitable means'. And we know too, for theoretical and historical reasons, that iambic is the quintessential meter for the greatest utterances in the English language. We only have to examine great poetry to find that – probably over 90% of it is in iambic meter. Furthermore, we also know that iambic pentameter, also called blank verse, has been the form that Shakespeare and Milton and Keats, to name three luminaries, have developed to a pitch of incredible power.

Here, then, is the challenge: how to write epic in blank verse? And the answer I discovered after 50 years of experimentation and reading is that you can't! Sorry, therefore, to be a slow learner. But Milton cannot be topped in the English language, and were one to attempt to write an epic in blank verse in English one would not be able to avoid slipping into the

Miltonic mode, as Keats found himself for all his ability. One would lose one's voice in other words, and write a pastiche Miltonic poem.

But does this mean epic poetry (admitting that there are epics in prose: The Lord of the Rings being a primary example) cannot be written in the English language? Clearly, I have to say, not! My own discovery was in what Dante had done. From a technical point of view, Paul Fussell's detection that 'The failure of terza rima to establish a tradition in English, as well as the general rarity of successful English three-line stanzas, suggests that stanzas of even- rather than odd-numbered lines are those that appeal most naturally to the Anglo-Saxon sensibility.' Put another way, yes, the English sensibility preferred patterns of 2 (the couplet), 4 (the ballad, quatrain, et. al.), 14 (the sonnet) and so on. But three-line stanzas were manifestly under-exploited. Moreover, Dante wrote in three-line stanzas, the terza rima, which he had invented and perfected in Italian; but this was not the case in English.

Pursuing this further, and studying examples from Dante lovers such as Shelley and his unfinished The Triumph of Life, I realised that not only was this iambic meter, but also the most brilliant format for driving forward a narrative: that the rhyming pattern – unlike Spenser's which creates a more static and pictorial type of poetry – propelled the story in a way (once one got the hang of it) that was truly amazing. In short, there was a way in which epic poetry in English could be written without seeming like another poet's work. I was following Dr Susan Rhodes' dictum: 'It's the ability to devise moves that adhere to the rules, but which are a novel adaptation that is the mark of a creative individual.' At least, I hope so: others will have to be the judge of it.

Finally, Dante not only provided me with the form, but also a way to access important content. Epics really are all about journeys to hell and back, however we arrange the topography. Odysseus, after all, literally visits hell, or Hades, but in a sense his whole journey from Troy to Ithaca – heck, from Ithaca to Troy, and then back again – is the journey of our life which necessitates, in all lives that are really lived, the visit to hell. As Jordan B Peterson commented, 'To suffer terribly and to know yourself as the cause: that is Hell'. Who really, then, is exempt from this? Only the facile, the comfortable, the self-deluded, though hell still has a special place for them; only they may not know or realise it.

The starting point, then, was my own descent into hell when I found myself with a malignant sarcoma back in 2011 and experienced three months in a local hospital. The treatment I had was fabulous – the nurses, the doctors were all models of kindness and concern. But however kind they are, hospital is a kind of hell – like a prison is. And you suffer; and around you, if it be any consolation, are those suffering even more; suffering even to death. You hear their cries and groans. Over the three months that I was in, I probably came to rest in at least 5 different wards; they all had their own peculiar flavour and atmosphere. I realised that the ward system could represent, loosely, the circles of hell that Dante describes.

As well, I realised that I wasn't a Roman Catholic, and not one who was going to be as precise as Dante about the gradations of damnation and of salvation; this was a spiritual and a psychological journey. It was a contemporary journey, not some slavish imitation. Yet it could incorporate many ideas from Dante. To take one example from the HellWard section of the poem: treachery was the ultimate sin for Dante, and I don't intellectually disagree with that assessment of its seriousness. However, for me and my experience in the modern world, the really serious sinners – when we go beyond our own personal offenders (as I do) – are (at the bottom of my hell) those thinkers who have been lauded in the West for corrupt and corrupting ideas that have influenced millions, and led them to leave desperate and often tragic lives as they fail to reach fulfilment or meaning.

So, here we are. We have completed volume 1, HellWard, of the three volume trilogy. The second volume will be 11 cantos covering the ascent of Mount Purgatory, and the final volume will be 11 cantos depicting the living Paradise. I had a glimpse of this latter state in hospital when an out of body, near death experience, came over me and I entered, albeit temporarily, bliss. This is the starting point described in Canto 1. Canto 1 is not part of hell properly, but the induction to it. In this way, each volume is 11 cantos long, but the induction in HellWard means there are 12 cantos. Therefore, the complete work will comprise 34 cantos. In numerological terms this is the number 7 (3+4). The perfect number which derives from combining 3, the number of the godhead, and 4, the number of Earth (as in the 4 compass points); in other words, the totality.

I am always interested in counting and looking at works from a numerological standpoint. Frankly, I was astonished to find, as I finished the final canto, that the total number of terza rima stanzas was 999. And those who have read my Mapping Motivation (Routledge) sequence of books will know that 9 is a highly significant number for all the work that

I do! Since I did not set out to do this, I can only regard it as a sign that I am on the right track and this work needs to be continued.

I hope you find it so and will want to discover what the modern hell is like, what purgatory, too, might be, and how finally we come to the light where our true selves are revealed in all their glory. Keep with me, then, as I undertake this journey – for me, for you.

James Sale

CANTO 1: HOSPITAL

The Argument:
The Poet finds himself in hospital with cancer and calls on Calliope, the Muse of epic poetry, to help him make sense of the modern world. In a Near-Death-Experience (NDE) he finds himself confronting an enormous force that creates and powers stars. In total despair and pain, the poet is invaded by this force at the point where the surgeon's knife went in and cut him; and so, unexpectedly, enters a state of paradise, albeit briefly; and from this moment he is enabled, and sent to enter all the Wards of hell to find the meaning of loss.

It had to be - that long descent began:
About me images, one century
That started, stuttered, showed how poor is man

In all things except his savagery.
My grandfather's face, first in that stale line,
Who missed the trenches through admin's mystery;

Was sent instead to fight in Palestine,
While friends he'd known all died in No-Man's-Land.
How lucky, then, for him; for me a sign:

1

Despite the misery, unintended, unplanned ₁₀
That characterised the fools who sought to build
A better world – progress – to make a stand,

As it were; as if politics could field
A force sufficient to overcome gods
Whose power, agencies were not like to yield

To mortal die, its throes and sadder odds.
Or, as if science, too, could weight outcomes –
Build Babels better far than Nimrod did.

Yet for all that building, they built one tomb
Called planet Earth – polluted, warmed and dying, ₂₀
Neglecting the while to study, exhume

The corpse of what the century was frying.
That long descent began. I saw myself as heir;
I saw myself for poetry is scrying –

Calliope come to me now, be here,
For I must tell how I came to that wild place
Where death is our doctrine, and twin despair.

For all this, know – each human hides that face
Divine, which is our task, within our will,
To reveal at last, if so by God's grace, ₃₀

That Love that Dante saw created hell,
And by His goodness covered Earth with stars,
So many, no mind could count them, they fill

The cosmos, yet hang so near us, yet far;
Our destiny, one day, perhaps, to cross
Over to where mortality can't mar,

Cast shadows, that prolong and deepen loss.
Calliope come now to me, epic queen:
Without inspiration, writing is dross;

Enable me to see what's not been seen $_{40}$
Before, but rise heroic to this quest
And find the Grail: what does this century mean?

And in so doing also find true rest –
The ninth heaven where Dante found himself,
Surprised and speechless, all light and all blest,

All one, yet being not somebody else:
Himself full-on, even as one snowflake
In dawn's deep drift, unique whilst still engulfed.

Calliope, Apollo's daughter, make
Me prophesy: you know what's to be,
You know the golden god and how he breaks $_{50}$

The proud. I came myself near history,
Despite a false summer then broken out,
Collapsing quite incomprehensibly.

Something medics came to see in my gut,
Something small, some shadow, should not be there,
But they'd remove – a snip – at most a cut

And I'd be well; there my life would be clear.
I waited hospitalised without sun,
No moon either, nothing natural, dear -

Gone without trace, as I went down, down, down: $_{60}$
One held my hand as anaesthetics did
Their graft - what was to do would soon be done;

And that malignancy within, well hid,
That choked, snake-like, intestinal flesh,
Would be revealed at last and I'd be rid

Of cancer's bloated presence and its wish:
Destruction absolute, assured, aligned –
Refusing life, wanting in death to mesh

With me, an apt image of evil's mind,
Small gains to build one vaulting emptiness, 70
At last undo what so much love designed.

What much love designed? And too was blessed?
Such sacredness I scarce can speak of – how
Before God now I tremble, quake, am less –

His glory. I saw it, as dying, slow,
Gutted of guts and lying on the bed,
Out of my body, sight soared to space, so

Effortlessly, and there I saw, ahead,
One giant finger turning candyfloss.
Wondering what -? I willed myself and sped 80

To see. There, close-up, I saw not chaos,
But its just opposite: not sugar wound
Around a finger, for which some child might fuss,

But a star formed in deep space, without sound,
No fanfare, tranquil; and the index bent,
One flick, it revelled forward on its round.

How could such power be – the whole cosmos rent
Into parts and each part on its own work,
And better still, each atom purposeful, sent

Whilst far below on a bed, injured, hurt, 90
Powerless to do evil, much less good,
I lay helpless, fit soon to be but dirt?

I choked, for knowing there's nothing I could
Do, racked on my bed of pity, undone,
Undoable. 'Lord, God!' My tears a flood

That nothing conscious might make or sum:
Only a baby in the night in pain
Hopes somehow something or someone must come

4

Because existence exists and – come again? –
Not only did He make the living ones, 100
He's Life itself, which means ... He is the plan.

I cried, 'Lord God, help me!' - and just the once -
Just as the finger turned, leisurely, out
Towards the void where all other stars shone,

And it seemed that He - the same He no doubt
Disturbs or interrupts - that that One might
Leave me forever stuck in my dark rut

Despairing, with those who mock without right,
Just then, before my thought caught my words' sense,
He turned, un-flexed, had me direct in sight 110

Before I could marshal the least defence
Even, discern my spirit from my soul,
Before I knew even my existence,

So fast, so instant, light itself seemed slow:
There, at the point the surgeon made his cut,
At that point exactly I felt God's blow

In me – so in me that nothing could stop
Its force, its flow and in one instant all changed,
As if mortality itself were shut

Off, and for it something brand new exchanged: 120
I mean that pain, in body and mind, ceased,
As suffering, past and present, was expunged,

And paradise abounded, total peace,
And more: His face I could not see, but rather
His presence, working within, me released.

But that was it – free – yet in me, together,
And I aware of some awful purity:
A whiteness of light, which recalling ever

I quake within, tremble before to Be,
Before such beauty as I cannot stand ₁₃₀
Before. So weeping, weeping endlessly,

Not tears as lost souls weep, you understand,
But joy at such happiness – profound, deep,
So deep nothing could undo, countermand,

Erase. At last my soul was in His keep –
And so He rocked me like a babe in arms,
The only time in three months I found sleep.

Nothing could interrupt that restorative calm:
No artificial light, blood tests, chit-chat
Or worse, the dying cries lacking love's balm ₁₄₀

In that hell of a hospital I was at,
Broke that deep sleep that God induced in me;
Till morning, sunlight at the window slats,

Waking to find, or know for certainty,
I was not bound to die, but yet to live,
For He had called me back, through His mercy,

All grace, unbounded, simply His to give.
The world strange, which not long before was not -
Altered; before, the busy bustling hive

Of bees circling till, exhausted and shot, ₁₅₀
They died in beds of blank indifference;
After, honey and overflow, the lot –

Time slowed to tripartite significance,
Future ahead, and present, a new past
In which what was random had His Presence,

Vital, pervading all moments, all mass,
Nothing beyond reaching beyond His reach,
That reach, and His hand, the net He had cast.

That net into which He too had been pitched.
No, not some distant god who lived remote, 160
Pulling the levers and strings, laughing as each

Man fell to common and singular notes
Of folly: no, not such a god as that,
Or some such Zeus on full sensual bloat,

Careless how the swan's neck proves Troy's mishap;
Instead, another God, and just the One,
Whose Word upholds all things, all changing shapes,

Till changing He Himself in flesh was done;
And now before me changes what's ahead
Beckons, a door, burning to drape upon 170

As if hanging, and hanging there my bed –
Out to deeper depths than this sick ward holds
And sinking at last the human cancer shed

If seeing my own horror and its toll
Might let light intrude, penetrate my soul.

CANTO 2: MOTHER

The **Argument:**
The Poet having survived the Near-Death Experience in hospital and having experienced the power that propels the stars and through it felt paradise, now sets off on his commission to go through all the Wards of hell. As he does so a companion appears beside him: Dante. Dante is the guide who has before been to all the dark places. Leading the Poet on, Dante takes him to the first Ward where the Poet meets someone Dante never met: his own mother in hell. The Poet's mother rejects him, and he tries to rescue her, but fails as he is too weak.

I knew then that I had to move, be gone;
Another depth beckoned. Daylight rose up,
Though bleached by how only bland neon shone.

About me busyness, but I was stuck:
Weak, as at least one third of guts removed,
How would I find my way – what grace or luck

Empowered, directed to what I craved?
And as I felt the dull ache return, so
Too someone beside me, someone I loved

Appeared. Though not met before, yet to know 10
Was easy: jaw pronounced, complexion dark,
But something more purely in spirit shows;

As if, imagining a distant bark
One plainly saw exactly the whole dog,
So now who he was was clear, and his work:

'Dante!' I cried, amazed, restraining sobs,
That sense of overwhelm at crisis points,
That sense of undeserving, yet through God

Just as cancer came, and its dark taint,
So now goodness abounded: Dante stood 20
Beside my bed, in death a living saint

For all he'd suffered, all he'd understood,
And beckoned me to join him on his way:
The way he knew before, if but I could.

'There is no time', he said. 'No time to stay.'
He gently smiled. I groaned within. So weak.
I'd much prefer to lie and chat and stay

And not get up. He knew and knew to speak:
'You wonder how I wrote my work and laughed
The while? Then what I did you too must seek. 30

My place in heaven, which for you I've left,
That is no sacrifice: to save a soul
From hell is worthy – are you man enough?'

He moved forward, hand grabbed mine, with one pull
Up, one arm round his shoulder, so we stepped
Together exit-bound, and with one will.

'The way up is down,' he said, 'you have slept
Too long.' No stars above, only dead light
Casting no shadows, in its shade we kept.

9

So slow our journey to the stairs' deep flight. ₄₀
We reached the balcony. I made to pause,
Hovering above the atrium, a kite-

like figure, scrying land, to spot what flaws
Of living things disrupt its still cover,
And last, perhaps, to find my strength and cause.

But he had none of it. 'Before it's over
There's one to meet, not as you met before.
Ward Two contains the start of all your bother.'

We reached the passage leading to the door
Left open, and no-one else seemed within. ₅₀
One bed, far-cornered, across lino-ed floor.

I heard soft murmurs, groans, and so ground thin
Existence barely able to register –
But as it did, alas, now was but a whine.

I saw a face as old as Methuselah,
But feminine instead. Eyes grey and dim,
Turning she mocked me: 'I know who you are,

And why you've come. You think you're friends with Him?
How little you know – look at me, look now!
He did this! And laughs, and why? For a whim. ₆₀

You think you're clever, son, but still you owe
Me, still you haven't paid me dues -' She stopped
Midway as if to choke, and I to know.

My hair electrified, raised up in shock;
My tongue cleaved to the roof of my mouth;
I could not speak, seemed my whole being locked,

For in her face I saw both horror, truth;
And he beside me could not bear the sight,
But hid himself awhile, and held aloof

From what his own hell lacked – a mother's slight. ₇₀
This Dante did not suffer, for all he did:
But I endured it – saw her lost in night,

Her loss-like rags screening what would be hid –
Beneath her clothes of care, and high concern,
Compassion's trinkets; there: her rings of pride.

For she knew best. And always had. So spurn
Advice from God Almighty, let Him try;
Yet, could He but see her, God too might learn;

And everyone who saw would see and pity,
Her mind reasoned. 'Who put me here?' she flamed ₈₀
A-sudden, and fierce, and then sadly, 'Why?'

'It's me. I am your son visiting, James'.
Her head lifted, but slow, as if her neck
Could scarcely hold the weight now I'd been named.

'Steven?' she said, in total disconnect.
'No, James, your first son'. Some deep groan emerged,
Giving me sense my being somehow wrecked

Her purpose she'd always been on the verge
Of doing – instead, I was there, her son,
An inconvenience not to be purged, ₉₀

A fact whose dreariness went on and on;
But, whatever, sons too had uses still,
And if no other, then torment was one.

How I longed, despite it all, just to feel
She loved me, and that deeply she approved;
My whole life waiting, and hoping she will

At last say words that mean, truly, I'm loved.
Instead, like serving stale but scalding tea,
She names the one we knew, with whom we lived

Those years: Gordon, husband who fathered me, ₁₀₀
'Do you remember him?' Could I forget?
How not recall that day's finality:

Him helpless, some jelly about to set,
And all living shivers shook out of him,
Arguing still as some shadow's dark net

Engulfed his light, I – but she stretched out a limb
To touch me – 'Bastard, wasn't he?' – her insult,
Casual and continuing to maintain her game.

How thick illusions are, how difficult
To penetrate; especially those we learn ₁₁₀
Sucking that milk which seemingly lacks all fault,

And we no brain that might express concern;
So grateful just to drink and thereby live.
How I felt her love, didn't doubt its turn.

On that basis, then, I was set to thrive,
Believing, as believe I did, her love
Was true, intrinsic, core and her real drive;

Belief, not knowing what I did not have,
As every step along her crazy way
Some subtle glitch revealed what forces drove ₁₂₀

Her soul to night, and so to skip the day.
Each one, decision, at each crucial point
Avoided conscience and its sharp display:

Instead, stood ready with a blunt 'I can't',
Or fond evasion, or bland platitude
Of 'Peace' she came to worship and anoint,

As if the word itself, and all its mood
Could trump all principles worth dying for:
Hail mother, you of right and rectitude!

What could I say? Already through death's door, *130*
My father, ahead in another ward,
Stuck like mother but on a lower floor.

'Yes, bastard,' she said. 'He's here too.' She paused,
As if bemused by her own intensity;
And I saw him dying, as his throat clawed

For oxygen, and his words hauntingly,
Futile and few, which gargled I made out
At last, hunched over him leaving me:

'Mudder, mudder, mudder ...' the word, no doubt
That drew me here now: his mother then, now *140*
My own, and its unresolved gunk and blight.

I tried to say, or at least make some show
Of positives: 'He's gone now, mum – no need
To fret yourself', but words would not allow

Release from pain: what was her past in deed,
Indeed, lived on, etched in flesh that could not
Forgive, forget, but held her in her bed,

Immobilised and fading, left to rot.
'Have you a son?' she asked, as if returning pain
To me, to think so easily forgot *150*

My precious ones, grandchildren got in vain
For her, if truly no memory served
To re-create them freshly in her brain.

I groaned within. Again, she'd touched my nerve;
And Dante who had shied away came back.
He touched my shoulder softly. 'You deserve,'

He said, 'more. Let's go. Why endure this flak?
Remember, here is where the lost convince
Themselves they're right, but with no going back.'

I heard his wisdom, and saw its evidence, *160*
But all the years, long years, being her son,
I wanted to save her, at last show my strength –

One last effort, one tug, it could be done.
She could, as if by magic, be released.
I turned to Dante. 'Help me, we are strong'.

I saw the sheets she sat in, how they creased
Around her body, encasing her, stuck.
'Let's move her from here, that way she finds peace'.

Like Herakles, seeing Theseus struck
Mute in that dumb chair on that long journey, *170*
So now I moved forward, still full of pluck;

But Dante stopped, for he knew more than me,
And watched as round my mother's arms I wrapped
My own and sought to lift her, break her free.

One heave, huge heave, and then the spell would snap;
She'd lift and from the bed, at last awake,
We'd talk, not like before, but in my lap

I'd cradle, whisper, tell her for her sake
Now had arrived and now she would be free -
The past was over, all its binding stake. *180*

How my mind, obsessed by these fantasies,
Worked mad, as up I felt her body come;
But then light drained, and flickered suddenly,

Ground shifted, trembling through some deeper thrum;
'Stop!' Dante cried. I felt her massive weight,
As upwards before, now my eyes stared down

To see her passive and in love with fate,
And those sheet folds around still clinging tight
Like coiling snakes who'd not discharge their freight

So much she loved them, and their toxic bite, 190
That God Himself – but then the plaster fell,
Showered our heads with dust and shattered bits –

Could not undo the hell of her free will.
No freedom now – I let her go – had to,
As Dante pulled me off, myself turned pale

And wretched – while she in all the hubbuboo
Stayed unconcerned, serene. 'Mother,' I tried
Once last time, as Dante made signs to go,

'See – One who made the world, and all the wide,
Who moves in everything, is everywhere, 200
Has made such beauty, but in us resides –

Our souls, mother, matter, for He cares.'
I wept, could not contain my tears. 'For most
Of all -' And Dante's hands, then, formed in prayer,

(He knew what must be said even to ghosts
And those who souls no longer live, adrift
From Him) ' – He's able to the uttermost

To save – to save, mother, only now lift
Your eyes and see light.' But her eyes were shut;
Ears too closing, of hearing too bereft. 210

'Call on His name,' I loudly shouted, but
To no avail. Some secret pleasure pursed
Her lips, some understanding I had not,

A moment; then blank and white, she turned, accursed
Away from me. I nearly – Dante caught
Me as I fell – fainted. Said he, 'We durst

Not stay a second more.' And so he brought
Me, space collapsing, out where ground stood firm.
No looking back. For now, no further thought:

She'd gone her way, and shown her true concern; ₂₂₀
But mercy led me: ahead, a darker turn.

CANTO 3: PUPIL

The Argument:
　　The Poet having escaped the relentless pressure of his mother's influence now enters the ward where he, surprisingly, meets an ex-Pupil he taught decades before. Someone extremely talented and able. But now the Poet realises that the Pupil – for all the learning that the Poet imparted back then – has gone profoundly astray and is playing with existence – with life itself. It's a deep shock, and the Poet recriminates with himself: had he failed to teach properly? But Nemesis closes in, which forces Dante and the Poet to flee through the hollow she has opened.

And now, if truth be told, I'd been unmanned:
My mother not able to recognise
Her son, or love him, except what she shammed.

The eerie passageway, so to my eyes,
Had some volume control – turned down a notch
Or two, but bass up louder – pitched red hues

Infesting air, and every breath would catch
Their resonance of kin. Imagine, then,

Some umbilical cord drawn through a crotch,

Constricted tight, unbreakable at both ends, *10*
And saturated through its skin with blood
No scissors, scalpel, knife could cut to mend.

'Hold me,' I wheezed to him beside me, good
And still my inspiration. As he did
The air came back, but worsening my mood:

My soul in living now wanted to hide
The shame of realising I could not
Love her (whom instinct, not soon denied)

Deemed 'mother'. Unnatural, then, or what?
Ingrate, then, after all she'd done for me? *20*
I, too, deserved her hell or deeper lot.

I was her son, perverse epitome,
Disfigured by all the guilt I held –
Which guilt burning like acid constantly.

Though dead seven hundred years, his arm I felt,
And wisdom from a deep life-giving spring,
Which balm calmed, countered all her acid spilt

So long ago – a sense of hope he'd bring,
Despite the depth to which my mother fell,
Despite her folly and endless feigning. *30*

'This modern world', he grimaced, 'truth to tell,
Is not the same as Florence was back then;
It's different, though stamped and marked as hell.

He paused, as if to weigh what that might mean.
'We knew what evil was, and how it caught
Unwary souls; but here ... you think you're clean,

As if deleting wrong were done by thought,

As if enough opinions made wrong right,
As if my way cancelled truly we ought ...'

He stopped. The strain of evil was not light. 40
How better to stay in God's heaven, free?
But now upfront, cries punctuating night,

We seemed on a ramp sloping listlessly
Down. 'Where is this place?' I shuddered; could smell
Bandages, blood, and splashed liberally

Some anti-septic wash which sought to quell
Or mask the stench pervading. Darkness, too,
Oppressed, diffused a red and putrid feel.

But sounds now, wailings, louder, I knew
What they were and that induced fresh dread. 50
'Yes,' Dante said. 'Your old friend waits for you.'

'But these are children's cries I hear ahead –
How could children be in a place like this?'
But before his answer formed, we stopped dead:

Ward Four. A narrow arch, brickwork a-mess,
And we stooping to enter its thin space.
Indeed, the more in, so it seemed the less

There was. Until, no room at all, a face,
Gaunt, bone-like, white peered through the red-rinsed
      dark.
'Hi James,' he said, emotionless and waste. 60

'I'd knew you'd find me; knew you'd like my work.'
What work? I thought. Then heard some sullen sobs:
The walls themselves had faces in, each hurt –

Each face half-formed, deformed, and like a yob's
Made so through lack of love and fatherhood,
But each one spoke, as one collective, mob;

Each one deprived of anything called good,
So each one cried and tried to finger-point,
But at what exactly my friend understood

And took some pleasure from, as every joint $_{70}$
In them strained to exit from their flat lives.
He was their monarch, reigning, they his runts.

'Kip.' I knew him well. But now? How time flies
And changes. 'What's done?' I queried. 'What's here?'
He swallowed, Adam's apple swollen, tied

And hard, as if words were something to fear.
Once, long before, he'd been my student, first,
Fluent in music, words, in meaning clear;

But what had seemed so promising, now had burst:
Youth's garnish stripped, removed, instead a husk $_{80}$
Remained, a shell suggesting what he'd lost.

So he began and justified his lust.
'Donations, James,' that's what this is about.
'I'm contributing; I'm someone they trust.'

'That's good, Kip,' I said, hesitant, 'no doubt.'
But what was it, despite fair-seeming words,
Made wincing within, chilling cold without?

I felt the good hand on my shoulder. He'd heard,
And understood intuitively. His grip
Though, for one so long dead, was over-hard. $_{90}$

Something appalled my guide, not some small blip,
But an enormity these yelping walls
Portrayed. 'After,' Kip said, 'curry and chips!'

'After what, Kip?' I pressed. 'I take their calls –
They need me, and the state has let them down.
We meet at a pub. I use a cubicle.

I'm reasonable, only 20 pounds;
It pays for travel and for grub.' He seemed
Pleased, while I'm perplexed. 'Call it a loan,

If you prefer; I give them what they've dreamed $_{100}$
Of.' As he paused, shell-shocked I realised
What he meant: the walled faces' contours screamed

Paternity – his, gotten otherwise
Than through the natural join of woman, man;
Children unknowing him, marked with his eyes,

Beget in a toilet, using his hand,
And passing on donations in a bag
For pennies and his vain, immortal brand.

How now he swelled with pride: not quite a shag,
But still he had achieved? To be a god – $_{120}$
Create life, more than others, so he bragged,

At least a brace, a score of kids – all odd –
But his whom lesbian mothers wanted most,
So much, they'd been no screening of his blood.

'Look!' he said, pointing, determined to boast:
'This one is mine.' A figure squirmed, outlined
Smooth on the wall, like in some Facebook post,

Where Kip tracked them, and kept hoping for signs:
Their mothers careless now of him, but not
Their kids – his DNA built their designs, $_{130}$

Their destinies: all they might have been – but -
Constrained to wonder, look and never catch
Their Pan-like father, his repeating shots

Creating replicas, not one a patch
On his original. As was. So sad
To see them straining now. And Kip to watch

And think this living; clearly all was mad,
And he reduced to such desperate straits:
His flesh itself his sickening source of trade,

Yet for so little recompense, small rate. ₁₄₀
I looked him in the face, but as I did
Hoping I could, by God's grace, communicate,

Tell him to quit, so the space, like some grid,
Contracted; the outlines more defined, squealed
Like pigs forced into a pen they'd have fled

Had they the sense their existence concealed,
Fatherless and lost. We stooped, we had to then,
As Kip, gaunter still, blocked my speech, and railed.

'I'm helping, giving my best, these women
Need me. No lectures, no sermons, from you ₁₅₀
Or Him, please!' 'But Kip,' I said, 'these children,

Abandoned so, they want, at least, to know,
And if they don't' - and here words failed within,
For some higher force wrenched my sense in tow

To His purpose – to prophesy, for shining
Invisible beside us now, Dante saw
What startled - stopping the yelping, whining;

As if they too, just once, could see the core
Of what was there: Apollo, golden youth,
Arrow now drawn from his limitless store, ₁₆₀

Bow bent in dread menace at poor Kip's mouth,
Hanging in front open, as if it sensed
Some dire presence but not perceived its truth.

'You will,' I said, and as I did I blanched,
So did the god run through me till my extremes
Lacked blood, and in my heart all avalanched

In frozen turmoil, 'never reach your dreams:
One of these whom you have begot, toyed with,
Will seek you out, find you, and be the worm

Undoing the fabric, the very stuff *170*
Of all you've built your life upon – be sure –
Apollo himself will plague you enough

Till even you, Kip, will cry out, No more.
These ants, gotten by you, will be your itch.'
He would have smirked, but clumsy, like a paw,

Involuntarily, he began to scratch
His face, and then his back, until his frame
Seemed raw, exposed, and each part now a-twitch.

He'd bred in deed to multiply his name
But each scratch skinned him further, till he was *180*
More skeletal, more red, yet not with shame.

As calculating what to say, he paused –
Our presence disruptive, not in control –
His voice an exhalation like a hiss.

'I know you knew me when I went to school
So long ago – teacher – but you don't know
How much I played my teachers all for fools.

None understood I had my way to go.
None got my beauty, got what I portrayed,
Or saw the hidden depths my work could show. *190*

None saw my heart-ache, none my fears allayed;
None, nobody, not One Himself got it;
And now, because of that, I've fully paid

My dues and I reject Him and His shit;
For I create and what invalidates?
See, see, yourself, around you, it all fits,

23

The cosmos mine and all is Kip's to take!'
His red, raw skin - and now his eyes burned red,
A-flame with energy defying fate.

But even as his words in molten shreds $_{200}$
Oozed out from his mouth, so the Ward shook
In one dire quake, and Kip spun round in dread:

For there was one at whom he could not look,
And she, severe now in her odd uniform,
Appeared through an opening the quake had struck

And strode towards him; and he, like some worm,
Twisted agonised against the flat screen –
One face yelped, 'Dad', surprised at Kip's return,

Demanding acknowledgement, where he'd been;
But Kip could only groan, as one might do $_{210}$
Who had to take the final medicine:

'Here you are,' the harpy seizing him cooed
With menace immeasurable. 'Remember me?
You raped me Kip, but I am not your food –

You owe me, and you owe my family.'
With that her talon-like grip round his neck
Pierced skin, and Kip shrieked, struggled, tried to flee.

'You owe me!' And her grip tightened, sought to break
All Kip's resistance. How his blood poured out –
The floor, the screen, himself plastered in streaks – $_{220}$

And we jumped back avoiding bubbling clots
Of gore that threatened to engulf us. Then,
My guide to me, almost having to shout

Above the din, 'If not now to go, when?
See the way the harpy forged in? That's our path
Out, down to all the futile grief of man.'

I knew at once to act; he spoke the truth.
Whilst Kip screamed bleeding, harpy carving pounds
Of flesh out of him in her bloody bath,

We dashed where the hollow opened, and round 230
Its corner till we were beyond that sound.

CANTO 4: BOSS

The Argument:
The Poet, appalled at the fate of a pupil he had taught, and how that pupil's life had become blighted, wasted, now enters another educational ward. Here he encounters a boss he had worked for many years ago: a man who specialised in that special form of hypocrisy whereby all friendly and helpful actions, along with the relevant jargon, conceal an underlying and pathological desire for control, recognition and self-aggrandisement.

And how I ran – in terror from those cries,
And in my heart of hearts the sense I'd failed,
And everything was breathless, full of lies,

Including my own life, until I stalled:
Collapsing, knee-caps cracking on the floor,
Lungs bursting, and all my balance derailed.

Only my guide's firm hand held me back, sure.
He waited, as I wailed and tried to grasp
What had happened – why? - a life in a sewer?

Why had I, his teacher, not done my task 10
Which is to teach, and introduce the good,
The true, the beautiful? If I'd been asked

Back then how I'd done, in all rectitude
I'd say I did well. But this? How far wrong
Can human beings go – he in manhood,

Me in thinking my example had been strong.
At last, my sobs subsiding, Dante said:
'Do not blame yourself; we all once were young,

But youth's no protection against the bad.'
I thought of England, how far fallen now. 20
Its education, the world it once led,

And in its place A-plus Stars, First Class shows,
Diplomas, tests, exams, all up for cash;
Vocations gone, careers the way to go:

Head teacher-in-just-five-years, make a splash;
Know nothing but lead the blind anyway,
Let learning stay rummaging in the trash.

So many skills equip us for today,
But knowledge and its greater counterpart,
Wisdom, where was that? Work? Yes. But play? 30

The mind a slave to idols without heart:
Kids sold a mess of pottage, futureless.
No music, drama, poetry, no art.

Within myself I felt a great weight press,
Constrain me, and a surging of despair
For all the lost souls, all the emptiness.

My guide felt so, and said, 'We must leave here.
Under heaven keep in mind what is true:
One gift the One who made all can't forswear -

Who, making the weave of being, can't undo - 40
I mean part of His divine nature is
Freedom of the will; we must share it too.

Love, then, created hell, allowed this mess
No order can reverse – for they refuse
It, preferring pain to another bliss.

Yes, Love made the gate here, framed the door we choose;
Love strong enough to fuel its own resistance,
Love -' and here, as if his ghost had lost its muse,

Dante, contemplating One's existence,
Was overwhelmed even in spirit – as 50
If ichor once more were subject to chance.

I felt him shaking – a tremor – that passed;
Then sober, sober as water from spring,
He said, 'To know the unbelievable is

To know -' but again, his voice was quavering,
'All those who tread this path still do His will,
Strive as they might to make some other thing.'

He would, perhaps, be contemplating still,
But some power woke him. He said, 'We must go.
There's One with whom we cannot force a deal.' 60

If contemplation had, a moment, slowed
Him then, now – like some match that's newly lit –
He flared up, urging me to the pitched road.

'Where to?' I said. 'You know: where there's less light.'
I followed in his steps, but lagged behind.
The shock of Kip had bruised with such a weight

I had to carry, process in my mind.
But darker yet the road ahead appeared,
And all the while I felt our path declined.

Its gradient shifting – ever down – steered 70
Us where unhallowed tiles absorbed the sound
Of footfalls landing with dulled, crude thuds. Weird.

Some echo - evil in intent to wound
By driving mad through its hypnotic beat
The careless soul enraptured by its round -

Surfaced, confident it too could create
Meaning from mimicking forward movement,
Not be its empty self, lifeless and flat.

So flat, there never could be improvement;
Hearing - dismayed body and sickened soul; 80
Was everything towards emptiness bent?

How doubt consumed me then, all being foul.
Where was goodness, and what my heart longed for?
Instead, my thoughts kept echoing: Is this all?

But reading my thoughts, Dante turned, knew more:
'If Adam had stayed true, in the garden stayed,
And we, too, without fault, observing law

Would happy gardeners be, his offspring made
To walk with angels in eternal sun;
There would be no darkness, no darker shade 90

As this sick ward to which we stagger on.
None.' Stopping, both his motion and his words,
He smiled at me. 'But look – at what is done!'

He waved, and I as one who hadn't heard,
Heard only groans, saw filth, and smelt the blood,
Of Adam's legacy which we all shared.

So Dante perplexed. 'Don't you see the good?'
How could I – this road to ruin's deep depths,
Aware of being's unbearable load,

And how at every stage each human wept? ₁₀₀
What good was there to see? And now a twist
Ahead I saw, where empty beds were kept

Awaiting restless souls who'd never rest;
And strange to note as well, not uniform:
Some large and bare and iron, others nests,

Small and comfortable. No one size the norm.
I quite forgot what good I was to see,
Intrigued instead, sure there'd be no harm

As I sought to speed up, be instantly
There. And as I sped ahead, through the door, ₁₁₀
A voice, acid and aside, greeted me.

I turned to see him glowering at the floor,
Or rather, as my focus grew acute,
He stared, bewitched, in bed, at shoes he wore!

So polished shiny black – only a suit
Was lacking, else the sense of his importance
Would be visible not just on his feet.

'Bryan!' I blurted out. He returned no glance.
His shoes held his gaze; I could not see why.
He spoke robotically, as one in trance, ₁₂₀

As one using words whose words are empty.
'Lie down, this bed here.' Without looking up
His arm gestured, casual, to one nearby,

The smallest of them all, that scarce would fit
My size. I hesitated – after all,
Why lie down now when guests might better sit?

His order, too – 'lie' – invoking control,
Made me uneasy, as did his fixed gaze
On shoes: what was it mesmerising his soul?

I noticed then ill-aspects bound to faze ₁₃₀
That hadn't first appeared to consciousness:
Each bed had – despite attempts to erase

Debris – slight remnants of surgical mess
Adhering, sticky plasters, blood clots, skin,
The horror of humans undone, undressed.

Minute traces maybe, but women, men
Had been here before, who had not got well.
I stopped my forward motion. 'Bryan, when

Did you get here? How long under this spell?'
I waited. Behind me I sensed my guide ₁₄₀
Arrive. Emboldened, 'Bryan,' I said, 'tell.'

Like some vicious swell of water, riptide,
Carried across his whole face in deep rage
As if I'd said something undignified

Offending him, like my presence upstaged
His own - with such an attitude he turned,
Determined to put me back in the cage

He once had held me in when his star burned
Across the educational wastelands
Of Christchurch and Hong Kong; with nothing learned ₁₅₀

By nobody. Headmaster of the bland –
The high-achieving parents' friend and aid -
All knowledge, like examinations, canned.

And I his deputy! I shivered, afraid;
Remembered what I'd tried to do back then;
How Bryan took credit for all I'd made.

But suddenly, a whisper, keeping in
His real intentions, hoarse - and his breath stank -
But nevertheless sounding like a friend,

'James,' he began, 'the school is at the brink, *160*
We need your expertise to reach new levels;
Together, what could we not achieve, think?'

Somehow his words – who can resist the devil? –
Had their effect; I found myself wavering.
Why not accept? Lie down now and be civil?

Play his game, not see his trap there, just hovering.
How weary now all seemed; I ached for rest –
A bed, duvet perhaps, or some covering.

I made to move towards – thought it best –
The shortened board, when suddenly Dante spoke *170*
Decisively: 'Stop, you are not his guest.

Remember how it felt before, his yoke?
So now consider what Procrustes did –
How many bodies, souls his tortures broke?

You were not made to fit this demon's bed,
But like great Theseus must break the breaker
Before you leave - 'and it was like some lid

Removed – his words - revealing in the beaker
The foul putrescence of that whole career;
Now, too, I saw a change in Bryan's features: *180*

Mr Reasonable no longer here;
Instead, he croaked with fiery venom: 'I'm
In charge' – spit curled up his lip, lined his leer.

But the effort all too much, he resumed
Abruptly staring back at his bright shoes;
As he did so, I saw at last his crime:

There, there, in the glass his own perfect view:
Himself, the peak and peacock of invention;
In love with himself, imagining his dues

In a perpetual cycle of willed intention. 190
I barely could contain my rage – the sight –
Evoking his erstwhile strictures and unction!

All those subtle distinctions: for him height –
His suit and manner, impeccable cant,
Babble; his own sense his own words had weight;

Of governing bodies supreme hierophant;
But now reflected in his own shoe-black
Only, the faintness of his own drab cult.

I broke. In one motion made to attack.
He flinched. Even his shoes could not compel 200
Attention as I raised my arm to whack

His head. A sound, uttered like some congealed
Squeal, of 'No! James!' issued from his throat,
And all his hidden fears surfaced, revealed.

The self-confidence and nauseous gloat
Gone. Now the little boy without his clothes
Lay there – utter nobody of no note.

My hand struck – struck all I had come to loathe,
And as I did two things jarred me, not him:
His head, not hard, but rather soft and smooth, 210

So that my blow slipped through his skull, as skin
And bone were absent, though he seemed to hurt;
But more, my anger, too, had turned to sin.

I stood shell-shocked, hand stuck in his vile dirt –
The sick imaginings of Bryan's brain,
Now with all its force seeking to subvert

My own resolve to be myself again,
Not some drone in his colony of schools.
But here my mentor saw my danger, pain.

33

'Your rushed anger has tripped you like a fool. 220
Stop struggling with your hand, and instead, think:
What teacher was it, principled and tall,

Who led you to waters where you could drink
Learning?' I felt hot poison up my arm
As Bryan's malice surged to do its thing.

J. E. Williams – he who did no harm;
He'd helped, gave me a chance, gave confidence;
Against all humbug he'd stood, kind yet firm,

And with him you knew, just knew, no pretence.
His image then, from so long, long ago 230
Formed in my mind, and as it did, so ice

Flowed torrential, an avalanche of snow,
To meet the poisonous heat, and quench it quite.
My hand snapped free – and Bryan slumped low,

While Dante caught my body's ricochet,
As stumbling back, we moved to get away.

CANTO 5: POET FRIEND

T**he Argument:**
Escaping from his ex-boss with his notorious and self-serving hypocrisy, the Poet enters a series of three wards in which he meets close personal 'friends' with whom he had once been close and intimate. The first of these is his 'poet friend'. Someone he once believed was truly inspired by the Muse, but now he learns is quite otherwise not inspired: how envy and rancour racked his life, and how his treatment of his paramour proves his undoing.

There was a door behind, which closed forever,
And I, despite the shock and overload,
Knew I'd escaped – just – finally to sever

The hold he had, the sense of something owed,
And guilt engendered by superior powers
On those below them. Now, another code

To live by. But where were we, and what hour?
Only ahead I saw a passageway,
Narrowly lit, narrow, sloping, dour:

All sunlight withdrawn, and time never day. 10
But still my mentor stood beside. I made
To move. He gestured otherwise to pray.

'The wound you have is serious,' he said,
'No man escapes without invoking grace.'
I dropped to my knees and raised arms to spread

Upwards. But that arm which had struck that face,
Felt all immobilised, except its heat's
Returning fever, rising in its haste.

To pray – ah, yes, truly, that's what I seek,
Or so I thought then, as one hand to other 20
Hand sought to press above the heart, and meet.

But no effort seemed to get me further.
I could not reconcile my own two sides:
Be one person, integrated, together.

The dark seemed darker still, the path less wide
We had to travel. Where were we going?
So-called learning proving one route to pride

And not much more: humans puffed up with knowing;
Not knowing exactly the hell they're in
Of endless iteration, pointless doing. 30

Then, Dante's hands reached out, and embraced mine,
As if by force he should join my split soul;
And as hands touched, by my heart, some divine

Surge rushed through and I regained control
Of my whole body; too, words on my lips
Formed a new kind of prayer, pure and full.

My arm repaired – motion and strength – hand gripped
With its old vigour. Waiting on the Lord,
Like eagles, they renew ... will never slip ...

In an instant I was up, keen to ford 40
The dark, which even now, as in response,
Thickened, so vision lessened more, proved hard.

My guide stepped forward, not subject to chance
Though groping, as he had to, for in this
Murk was no other way we could advance.

So slowly, hands feeling, keen not to miss
Each step they guided. Our voices kept touch;
So I asked him why he'd come, left his bliss

For me. At last he spoke, but said not much:
'I wandered too, was lost, in a dark wood, 50
As you now in this hospital's cruel clutch,

But there is one who names your name, names for good,
Who in her heart of hearts is pure, and stands
Before the One, though yet she is not dead,

But her heart working ceaselessly commends
You, which as prayer, total in belief,
Before that very throne achieves its end.

Through her, Beatrice ordered your relief.'
I gasped, breathless, like my life emptied out,
And for an instant my heart shed all its grief 60

For she loved me, loved me still, and no doubt:
Love lights, and love cannot be overcome
Because beauty stops motion at its root -

So her face shone through like a wave's white foam
Flushing the bleak sea of its deepest black;
But there, almost there, I saw them, alone,

Working their weird ministry together, stuck
Beside the wall, but Ginty in the bed
And Marlene tending him, though she was sick

While he had health, apart, that is, from needs 70
That plagued his mind in its eternal torment.
She drank – a lot – and asked when they'd be wed?

Her voice, a whine, why had he been so absent?
He feigned concern, his voice beguiling, soft,
Revealing nothing like his real intent.

I saw his eyes twitch, and his father's ghost
Haunt his every calculation – his Will.
To marry Marlene? Inheritance lost!

But she must be led, held constant to him still.
Another drink then? He proffered, she quaffed, 80
They laughed, though she sounding desperate, shrill,

And he insincere, with a phoney laugh
Becoming a nasal snort, jackass style,
Yet through it something else, some other stuff

Wanted to surface and be known the while.
How the laughter slowly dimmed; they aware
Increasingly, that no laughter, no smile

Removed them one jot from just where they were.
And now the light that my love's face had lit
Began to dim, as nothing here would cure 90

Pain, for like Jason before, whom Medea's wit
Finally destroyed in a double act,
So Ginty now discovered his own pit.

'Don't leave me.' How fragile, then, his pact
With her. She drank the more, while his smile drained.
'Please don't go,' he begged her, as his voice cracked.

'Please!' His hand reached out, fumbling, old and veined,
Attempting some connection never had,
And she immobile, drunk, looked and disdained

Him now. 'You don't know grief – or where it's hid, *100*
Do you Ginty? But wait till you are old,
Then, then ... you will remember what I said.'

He whimpered; though in bed, how he felt cold,
How nothing was as it might be. But then,
Aware he'd been observed with too much told,

He stopped, let go of her, let go of pain.
'James!' he guffawed, his beady eyes on me
Fixed, and computing, as they did their scan,

Who was the other, why did they walk free?
'What brings you here?' he ventured, laughing as *110*
To indicate just how nonchalantly,

Careless, in the depths, all was between us.
And all the while, Marlene ignored, drank more.
'A mutual friend,' I said, 'brought me: The Muse,

Remember her? She got me through the door.
Beside me, too, the master whom she sent
To lead beyond this waste to better shores.

Dante, you know?' His eyes made a sharp squint,
With a sharper intake still, not his breath
But soul contracting into its sharpest flint *120*

Of being, severing any belief,
For, visibly, Dante diminished him.
Still, whatever, he needs must hide his stress.

'Of course, I know the Muse, wrote poems,
Just like you Dante; Oxford man, you know.
With Heaney, others, we were all at Magdalen.

Poor James, who doesn't know Handy, I do.'
He paused, looking for signs: was Dante won
Over? 'To which college, James, did you go?'

'A small place, Ginty, small place, but my own; *130*
There I began the work, small work, small steps,
But each one, in faith, I trust takes me home.'

A sadness swept me, not words from his lips
Only, but that I desired to reply
At all, since I'd thought that we shared friendship.

As that thought struck, another quality
Re-masked Ginty's face, this time a jeer:
'Does Dante know I'm now an O.B.E.?

Who cares for poetry? It's nothing here.'
And as he said those very words, deep down *140*
Something changed – like some thermometer's

Rising mercury hitting red; Ginty's frown
I can't forget, and Dante's arm about
My shoulder, hugging me like his true son;

And Marlene's hair, once red, now growing shoots
Of flecked and flecking grey, like fine, foamed froth,
Spun off from her head, as some snake might spit.

'Turn,' my mentor said. 'He has denied truth;
On this you cannot look, but see my chest?'
He pointed, and there I saw his cloak's brooch *150*

Absorbing silver and mirror polished;
And so I came to see Ginty, reversed
In image, friend as was, on Dante's breast:

Medusa petrifying one she cursed,
All serpents of hell alive in her stare,
Withering, tense as a bladder to burst;

He howled once, clutched a heart that wasn't there,
Rolled backwards, helpless, like a dropped stone
Till stopped in his own horror's frozen fear.

'Run', Dante said, 'run! Flee Medusa's zone.' *160*
With that, his hands snapped tight as shielding screens
Across my eyes and swung, then shoved me down

The way, so that my head swayed, lost it means
Of balance in trying to run; almost
I fell, but Dante's strength held me - a beam

Upon which I depended, though a ghost.
How could that be? And too, how could a friend
Betray all we stood for, and our shared past?

But now my lungs felt under diver's bends
And I could barely hold the strain. He, though, *170*
Sensing collapse, but danger at an end,

Ceased running. Hands slipped loose, and I saw now
Only more darkness, felt invasive cold,
As marble in winter, entombed in snow,

Despite the running hard as I could,
But such heat now seemed scant, a candle's worth
Perhaps, to light a blackness dense as old,

Settled as a crust over all the Earth,
Unbreakable. Despair welled up inside.
'Where are you, my friend?' I cried out in grief; *180*

It seemed to me that all my friendships lied.
What was this corridor, where were the true
Ones? But then Dante's voice rose, took the lead,

Cutting the murk: 'Now learn what liars do.'
Though I could not see him speak, yet how proud
And certain his voice rang, and then I knew

The folly I had followed lacking doubts,
Thinking I had friends untested the while
And here discovering for myself their roots.

Whether his voice, or my thoughts, sharpened wile, *190*
But somehow the way ahead seemed to clear.
Though dark still, the path stretched it seemed, for miles.

Slowly, laborious, we made our way where,
For sure, false friends pretended love, disguised
Their baser motives with bland cant of care.

Which meant ahead was dread of what I despised:
To meet ones I'd loved, and shared once a bond,
And so to see them fresh, with different eyes.

All sickness now, that then was sweet and fond;
I prayed protection, grace to leave this land. *200*

CANTO 6: COLLEGE FRIEND

The **Argument:**
    The Poet, having visited the HellWard of his false poet friend and witnessed the punishment this friend's own consort deals out to him, now arrives in the ward where another friend, Saul, going back even further in time to college days, resides. Here he encounters all the old repetitive and competitive spirit by which Saul sought to dominate and humiliate other people. But treating people this way proves no sound basis for life, as Saul discovers.

> *But such protection as I wanted then*
> *Was not to be in this zone I was in,*
> *Heavy as it was with the stench of men,*
>
> *And human nature starved of love, and thin,*
> *Deprived, denied, denying, wholly set*
> *On self-assertion, at all costs, to win.*
>
> *And these, it seemed, my friends, or once were that.*
> *Remember, I thought, how David once had*
> *His Jonathan: two souls which truly met*

Beyond the love of women, if that could ₁₀
Be – which, after all, I didn't think so,
For man needed woman not to be mad.

As I thought this, another thought came too,
But from a deeper source, a different place,
And not my head, which knew it didn't know;

Instead, my heart, a star formed with a face,
Shining with brilliance that purified,
So that I paused, dumbstruck, with grace on grace.

Thus Dante turned, to see me, who had died
Almost, but now the corridor was lit ₂₀
Ahead from light my own being supplied.

'Know,' Dante said, 'the grace is all of it;
To waver one moment is to quench this flame
Which out of you now flickers but a bit.

Imagine when, finally, we have come
Beyond this lair to where your true love is,
There you'll find the white stone that has your name.

At that point only, life, and you will live.'
I heard his words, and more hope flared within
A while, but then, more sanguine, took a dive ₃₀

As grace felt lost, as if submerged by time,
And darkness held its sway again. But still
I felt his presence closer now: the friend, him

Who'd been before, and for my sake made trial
Once more. So courage, too, I found makes light
As we moved on, the dark seemed less the while.

We passed stale products of sickness, its plight –
Abandoned mattresses, stacked to the walls,
Sheets, pillows, surgical objects of rite,

A litter of rubbish, till a small hall $_{40}$
Opened, and within, slight three-sided screens,
Each one a world for someone and their gall,

Aligned themselves, contained a space, a scene
Playing a future contained in each past.
From one smoke rose in waves of nicotine.

I heard a sloven-cough; perhaps to ask
Would be polite, but something in the sound
Alerted me. Who was it I'd unmask?

Like some consultant doing his ward round,
Stepping aside from Dante as I did, $_{50}$
I drew the curtain – there, splayed on the ground,

Bed vacant, Saul sat, listless and sad,
Beside a heap of empty bottles, cans,
Dead fags and packets, litanies of bad

Habits that litter earth like specks of sand,
Sterile in their numberless magnitude,
And here they were laid out, as if a plan,

As if he'd thought, for him – Saul - this was food.
How wasted, grey, he looked, and dozily
Now, eyeing me, confused, not sure what mood $_{60}$

Best served his purpose, but veering to frosty;
Curtly, he addressed me: 'James,' his speech slurred,
'What took you so long? You'll never beat me.'

With that, so satisfied with what he'd heard,
Namely, his own voice, he took a long swig.
He'd beaten me to hell, as he preferred

To be the winner, and I simply to shrug,
As back then, long ago, I had; ignored
The evidence of every action's thuggery;

And how he'd swerve to crush whatever soared 70
In human spirit without benefit
To him – because for him all hope despaired,

And none must be allowed their faith in it.
No hope, no faith, and now in hell, no love;
No understanding either I don't fit

This place; my passing is through and from above,
Which is what he will not and cannot see,
Acknowledge what I – always through grace – have:

That soul's original identity,
That likeness whereby what was to begin 80
Impressed its properties on you, on me,

Which was not love, not power, and sure not knowing,
For what flashed forth created, made pure light
In one decisive call, one final showing

Of creativity and its delight:
Remember? How my soul aches for that state
Again – and as I thought so, so my bright-

-ness glowed once more. Saul blinked, disconsolate,
Blinded, unsure what such a surge might mean;
But bitterness, aware his own dark fate 90

Around him, lost without a single gleam,
Retorted in his rage: 'You never will,
James, never; for what you have's never been

Creative!' Then saying so, took a swill,
And a long satisfied sigh from his sup,
Almost a burp, emerged, then all was still.

I stood transfixed awhile, tortured and strapped
To the terrible torment of his words,
Which, supposing they were true, wounded and racked

My soul; as long ago – playing - the Bard 100
Before the king felt the full force of spear
Attempt to fix him there, take him off-guard,

Undo ten thousand things he'd done; I swear
Pure jealousy, but worst of all – the text
Made clear, the One Saul sought was nowhere near;

Indeed, to Saul was now a disconnect
That never again would power his life
For good, but through the Endor Witch would vex

Him bitterly, and lead him to his grief.
Now my own Saul sat drunk and speaking hard 110
Words trained at killing, cutting as a knife.

My soul – this friend of mine: what had I heard?
Judgement curbing all my possibilities,
Destined to be with my own past interred

Forever; to end like him, he like me,
And this the game, end-game, that was his aim;
No friendship, then, in this, but company

To join him in the Ward, and blot my name.
Knowing, believing so fulfilled itself;
Standing there already too long a time 120

I felt paralysis creeping through half
My frame. I looked down, forced myself to view
His face. There, a slight smile, almost a laugh -

Like one I saw invade, immerse, imbue
My mother's face when I escaped, but just,
Her Ward - creased his lips, for now he knew

His power, as mine diminished, light gone bust;
But feeling less, my torso now felt more,
Like blisters erupting, liquid, then crust,

Hardening my skin to scales, inward to core. 130
As it did, diminishment taking hold,
So he abruptly staggered from the floor,

No longer mild and mocking drunk, but bold,
A giant whose face contorted with bleak rage,
Like Polyphemous, I trapped in his fold.

Two eyes became one nothing would assuage
Except my whole being join him in hell.
Like some rookie actor on the big stage

As the lights go up, no longer feels well
And suddenly freezes in the spotlight, 140
Spectators expecting, but not this spell,

So now, frozen in myself, and in blight,
Unable to resist, Saul reaches out;
His touch means not hello, more like goodnight.

My scales already grey, and grey as grout,
Render me brick-like, rigid as a stack,
Astonied by friendship rooted in doubt

And having come this far, no going back.
I try to parry, raising my left hand,
Which moves like some ant in glue, straining, stuck. 150

As in slo-mo, each move can scarce expand;
Whilst his are brisker, faster than a fish
Whisking away from danger nearing land.

He grabs my index finger; with one crush
I hear it crack and how I howl with pain;
'Like me,' he grins, 'Not brick, but feel your flesh!'

His grin a grimace with more threat in train:
What next? His beer-breath right up in my face;
I addled with a hard-boiled egg for brain.

How fears come on us – so rooted in place, 160
Defence impossible. Who am I now?
To be here, lost, and die, without a trace

As atheists – as those who never know
The truth. What white stone, then, might I inherit?
What place left for me, so fallen, so low

And utterly without virtue, merit?
My knees folded downwards, as he above
Me waxed immense and vaunted victory, credit.

'You see,' he cried, eyes blazing, him the guv,
'You thought you were so clever, didn't ya James? 170
You didn't reckon on how strong I'd prove:

Yea, me, you dumb pillock, and Saul's my name!'
His two thumbs raised, about to plop my eyes
And leave me blinded with him, and in shame.

But as his thumbs rose, and all seemed goodbye,
Yet there in the corner Dante stood, and smiled -
Like ... not even bothering. My mind thought, Why?

He'd been my mentor, father to this child,
So how observe now my blinding this way?
Why? Why? The question's self just drove me wild 180

And as I raged within, so without the clay -
Cement I had become - became aware
Of something, not thing, living, and in play;

So that Saul's thumbs seemed suspended, set there,
And I at last in the wide interval
Unfroze and found myself creating prayer.

The word – the name came – some power spiritual
That Saul could not imagine or conjure.
The floor sliding, sloping back to hell,

A deeper hell than we were in, for sure, _190_
And Saul's footing slipped. His face went berserk,
Demonic, wanting to have me secure,

To put me down beneath a thicker murk
Or deeper depth than his own blackness owned;
No glory shines there, and no goodness works.

As from my knees, grace strengthened me to stand,
I saw his fear twofold: envy unsatisfied -
Finally, not to have me as he planned;

But worse, the tilting floor, opening wide
A hole behind him with no seeming base, _200_
Where those denying others were denied.

There it was: pure panic blotching Saul's face;
Now Dante moved, as I tilting headlong,
Weakened by Saul, and nowhere there was safe.

First, bed and screens toppled, like matchsticks flung
Into a dark bin, then disappeared, gone!
But Dante saved me, one word on his tongue:

'Jump!' Which I did, with all I could summon;
Yet twisting, as I did, having to turn
To see one last time Saul gripped by his daemon. _210_

There, hair uprising in its grey-permed burn,
Eyes blood-shot wide, erasing all his whites,
Mouth shifting from curse to some mad mute mourn.

His body half-floating, held like a kite,
Some upward draught, then down, and lost in night.

CANTO 7: SCHOOL FRIEND

T he **Argument:**
The Poet, saved by a whisker of prayer from his violent and unstable college friend, Saul, now goes even deeper, down to a school friend from 50 years before. Here he finds himself in a web of friendship with darker designs on what friendship means, which is the undermining of morality itself - a deep chaos that Dobbin seeks. The goddess Pallas Athene rescues the Poet and restores Diké to her proper place. Like Arachne, Dobbin is unable to overcome the goddess.

I scarcely could consider what I'd seen
And what the upshot was, as then I crashed,
Sprawled on a hard floor, left finger broken

And throbbing violently, cracked and crushed
By Saul's attack; ribs too now bruised and aching;
Breath short and desperate; adrenaline rushed

Throughout my body; mind unfocused, creaking
With strain; and spirit lacking force and drive;
The years, long years, of friendship and its faking

Brought my life down till I was bare alive. ₁₀
Around me darkness, black as a coal seam;
My thoughts were all, 'Where am I?' And, 'How leave?'

'Where is my guide?' Was that someone I dreamed?
How lonely being lonely felt. Almost
False friends were better, comradeship with them

Surely counted, at least together not lost,
As lost now and in darkness blinded, bound
By fears and the tingling creep of dead ghosts?

I shuddered; perhaps if I made a sound
Someone would come. But no sound came. Only, ₂₀
Within, a pulse, flawed, as if it were wounded

And at the last would stutter, stop my journey;
I, then, the one who comes to see too late
The joyless depths of friendships which are phoney.

Sightless and soundless, bounded in my wait,
How long I do not know, but then his touch:
Some spirit bled fresh from him changed my state.

Within I felt my heart glow, and with such
A luminosity words were released,
But not before my tears of self-reproach. ₃₀

"Teacher," I said, "and more than teacher: priest
To whom I confess, who knows how I have failed,
How in the moral realm I rank the least,

Because all righteous tracks I have derailed -
My soul, I mean." And as I said the word, 'soul',
I felt a tremor - like naming detailed

Its nature, leaking essence in its spill -
So small, at least it seemed the word I spoke,
But then a wave so strong it flushed my ill

And for a moment as it passed, I woke: 40
Myself became visible to myself,
Not a mere image in a rippling lake,

As if my eye without glass, in triumph,
Could see itself and everything be known,
So transparent each human heart, each Seraph

Also; although in the centre there's One
I could not fathom in that instant clear.
Then, as I tried, my seeing was undone.

Instead, beside my mentor, in the drear
Backdrop of the hospital I stood drained. 50
"Help me understand," I said, and old fear

That had always been with me, once again
Assailed. I barely thought continuing
Possible; my words failed, eyes begged explain.

But Dante knew my thoughts, knew everything,
And his voice I noticed as he began
To speak was like the sound of one who sings,

Entrancing in its range, breath-taking span,
As if in its pitch the whole universe
Resonated with one frequency, man. 60

"Each thought you have, and each desire you nurse,"
He said, "derives from dreams and dreaming's air,
And from this invisible and primal source

What's solid materialises here;
In mortal life cause and effect may not
Always manifest as a conjoined pair;

Delay can be profound, prolonged, such that
The superficial mock, see that as proof
No order is, or word established fiat;

Such ones also mocked Noah and the roof $_{70}$
He built whilst all the summer sun once shone;
But where we are we find a different truth:

How in the past Saul had you overcome;
And so his ghost, which you believed was real,
Believing so gave him the power to stun

Your being and render you vulnerable
To his assault, as your wounds testify.
But put away the pain and shame you feel,

For we're not done, and you must fortify
Yourself against greater enemies yet; $_{80}$
Raw strength Saul had, but stronger still's the lie."

He paused, as if to magnify effect,
And I in wonder thought who he might mean.
"There is someone near", he said, "you must meet.

So let us go." The fear no longer seemed
As real; his arm swept me forward as some
Father encourages his child who's been

Unable to stand, but once standing's done
The child will walk. So I, with surety,
Found myself now and able to move on. $_{90}$

The darkness began to dim, and I could see:
Our corridor had rooms on either side
And Dante knew where he was leading me.

We came to a door unlike – wider and white –
Others we had been through before; as well,
Already open as if to invite

Lost tourists to enter, enjoy its spell
Of kind furnishings, not like the bare beds
And well-worn basics' catastrophic sprawl

I'd seen before. There, sitting upright, head _100_
Reclined, yet so relaxed - and smiling hard
As if to greet - this friend I knew was dead.

"Dobbin," I said, uncomfortable, "I heard
Word you ..." But what I wanted to say then
I struggled to, for how was death a word

In this extremity? But he began
All soft, inviting, and saying, "So kind
You came; I'd hoped some time that you'd drop in;

You know, my friend, there's so much on my mind,
Since last we met – when was it? – '81? _110_
Remember, Shakespeare, and his Tempest lines?

A turn or two we walked, till talking done
And all the world we set to rights; and right
Our friendship. Remember? How we went on?"

How we did indeed, and his voice, so slight
Now; yet with its mesmeric melody
I heard, and all its underlying wit.

The set-up was: he somehow leading me,
For I could not constrain his genius,
Or guess at how profound he felt his envy; _120_

My task to let all negativity pass.
Good times: the mind centres on them, forgets
Perhaps, what happened then, happens, alas.

He stirred, and stood, as I did by the sheets,
And Dante, who'd pressed me so hard, now seemed
Away the while my past found sharp repeats.

Recalling, as memory's self its self's a dream,
In Wales, both students, he my visitor,
He came to my room and – I heard my name:

55

"Jim, let's move on." He pushed the black wheelchair ₁₃₀
Forward, and I, confused a moment, losing
That recollection I had had, (but where?)

Slumped downwards in the carriage he was choosing.
From patient to porter, now this porter led.
How quickly out the door, speedily moving,

Away from recovery and his bed.
That was it; that was where he had proposed
We tie our knot – and I be in his web.

I felt a shock – we had wives! – still I dozed,
As through another convoluted twist ₁₄₀
And turn of reason he pressed, soft voice glozed

About the something he desired exist.
Imagine: silence then, and the sun shines
Transparently through threads strong as a fist,

But thinner than a smear of fine white wine.
So I, his labyrinth in and its round,
Approaching where the spider claims, "You're mine.

Experiment! Our friendship's on new ground."
Bolt upright in the black chair, now awake,
Aware that webs, like water, run profound ₁₅₀

And there's an object that the spider seeks.
Arachne's tapestry – lo! – what she weaves:
Majestic, though hubris guides all she makes.

Caught there, now watching how gods really live:
Inflamed by passion and the world well lost
If mortal flesh might have the thing they crave.

I saw young Ganymede and Zeus's lust –
How boyhood never grew to man; instead,
Eternity (his) spent in filling cups;

I saw Apollo, before he grieved blood ₁₆₀
Of Hyacinthus, with him so blent
And all proportion absent in their bed.

Even Achilles, hiding in a tent,
I saw: Patroclus, unmanning him there,
Ensuring destinies to which they went.

And more beside I saw, and had to stare
At each outrageous, hyperbolic act,
Sterile as lava, as hot and as bare.

Then where (I asked myself) stuck as a fact
On Dobbin's filigree, was Dante now? ₁₇₀
Mesmerised, who'd relieve me from this trap?

I felt a hand; saw - like pasted on shadow -
Eye whites and the gleam of teeth emerging
For consummation I was bound to follow.

Yet too a voice, soft as a vow of a virgin,
Some susurration holy from no place
At all, but vital with relentless urging

Possessed me, just as Dobbin's lips and face
So closed on me I smelt his breath's stale rank,
Aware I was just seconds from his embrace - ₁₈₀

A lost coin dropped in his bottomless tank.
But whatever tapestry was before
Another shone from which the other shrank

In fear – for her – (in truth that one) – I saw:
The one not born as others, but who sprang
Armoured and fully-wise, without a flaw;

Of whom the whole cosmos in chorus sang
Her praises, as before her aegis held
The Gorgon, from whose face fear itself hung -

Aloft, whose spear which only she could wield ₁₉₀
Would penetrate beyond the body's corpse
And drive to where the human soul is killed.

Truth is, I'd failed and my whole being lapsed,
Was lapsing, sauntering to easy street,
Willing the hero within be eclipsed;

So I with mediocrity might meet
And flow across the bridge with one and all
Who end their lives with just one word: defeat.

But as she loved Odysseus, who heard her call,
So now I heard but lowered the while my eyes, ₂₀₀
For seeing such purity meant I'd fall -

Unworthy me without a sacrifice –
The goddess stirring ashes of my heart,
Blinding my sight from that which petrifies:

Her shield. 'Great Pallas,' I, sweating with hurt,
'Undo this veil and show me what you weave;
So long I've longed for your immortal art

Besides which none of man exists or lives:
Show me', I cried, 'What you do, who you are.'
Still my eyes held down, inward to grieve; ₂₁₀

For how slow, and outwardly from afar
She was, unlike Dobbin who now seemed close,
Almost upon me. But then I heard her:

A thrill of hope ran through, for all my woes;
Though blind, time stopped - as Dobbin froze and stalled;
My mind's eye saw her spear shuttle and sew

A pattern that first looked baseless and scrawled
As if some infant did it and not better,
As if thin air itself held form which failed.

58

But then as longer I looked some new matter ₂₂₀
Appeared as some deep imprint in my soul:
Some web, so intricate, I could not utter

Exactly, or really describe at all;
Only the goddess Diké's name flashed forth
And lit the darkness, breaking Dobbin's spell.

Diké! The universe admired her worth;
Deathless Athene pledged to fight her cause
That justice might prevail over the Earth,

Above and under. Time resumed its laws;
Dobbin slumped back, exhausted with effort, ₂₃₀
Unknowing still why now he'd come to pause

And not achieve the goal he'd craved and sought.
In one moment I saw his pupils narrow,
Saw all his eloquence reduced to nought.

Like some ghost receding, fast as an arrow,
He went from me, and his black chair withdrew,
So I collapsed as if hit by his blow.

On the cold floor I lay, unconscious, raw,
Until I felt the arms of one I knew.

CANTO 8: NEIGHBOUR MURDERER

The Argument:
The Poet, disgusted with three false friends from different stages of his life, now struggles further downwards where he finds an ex-neighbour of his who murdered his own wife. The relationship with this neighbour is not close, as with previous friends, but the proximity of their house is horrifying, as is the nature of the crime: not just murder but the depths of the betrayal involved. And for what? Sordid cash from an insurance policy.

I staggered upwards as his arms held me,
Sobbing and cold, yet grateful too for what
I'd seen though blinded, for still I was free

From Dobbin's tentacles, dark webs, hard knots.
Forward we went, as backwards into depths
Of nothing Dobbin floundered, quite, quite lost,

Invisible now and wholly without strength.
But he who was beside me, him I knew,
The poet, whose words were power and truth.

Confused, my sight still faltering in its view, *10*
'I owe you everything,' I said, 'but where –
As Dobbin charmed me with his guile – were you?'

How stern, then, Dante, in his might, appeared
To me: I simply, beside him, a child.
Yet still he answered, tone blistering, sere.

'You know your being is to be defiled,
So why require the master intercede
On your behalf, or block what you self-willed?

There comes a time when overwhelming need
Dictates my force is given leave to play. *20*
But here your own corruption plays indeed;

Real heroes determine, make their true way,
Which you so failed to do. And yet -' his voice
Then faltered, as lost in some profound amaze –

'And yet I saw, as you, especial grace
Which Diké forms: the fabric of the world,
Before which evil turns blind and goes hoarse,

As wisdom – beautiful! – is thus revealed,
Though your eyes were barely lifted to see,
Mine own Athene's glory lit up, filled. *30*

Heaven, though you remain in misery,
Cannot be held in check, restrained or stopped,
And I was where forever I must be

Despite how far this place we share has dropped.'
If I'd felt bad before, his words now scourged
My vital spirits, flayed all I had hoped

About myself, my being, so not purged
Of all its predilection for huge ill;
The universe was no song now, but dirged

Along in faltering steps until it fell ₄₀
Into some silence too scary even
To contemplate, much less witness at all,

As I did now – the absence of that heaven.
But Dante saw my distress; and pity flows,
Though we do not see its power till it's proven -

Until the balm's applied that heals the blow.
'Myself, like you, was once all strut and pride,
Could look unmoved on what went on below,

Not sensing in my soul what it would hide;
But those who seek salvation simply must ₅₀
Face every deception to which they're tied;

There is no other way – ahead, the dust
Awaits, and before you sense its covering
Divest yourself of greed and pride and lust.

Look deep, my son, your weeds are there, flowering;
But where you go, if there you truly want -
Your heart must find the seeds of love's real gathering -

For that's the antidote for all rank plants,
Such that you'll weep to even think of them,
While thinking cuts itself to end up blunt.' ₆₀

So said my master, and I heeded him.
We descended now a stairwell, polished, smooth;
Smooth to the touch, but touching congealed phlegm -

Like nacre in its coating, hard but proof
That all that glitters is not pearl or gold,
For within this coating the core was wrath;

And as I thought of it my blood went cold.
Arriving at a corridor just like
That alley leading to the underworld

Where neighbours we'd known and seen in the light $_{70}$
Toiled in their way across the cut dividing
Our properties - the lines defining right -

There I recalled that strange and disobliging
Phenomena: houses round, posh and neat,
And yet each day, for some years, rubbish lying,

Dumped and deliberate, littering the street,
Put down, like defecation in the dark,
Soiling the living, where they meet, for spite.

The mess. The filth. Then I came to his ward,
And peering in saw Peter there, austere, $_{80}$
Preoccupied, as hiding – what? – more fraud?

And muffled sounds, stifled, a boot parked there
From which some long agony, enclosed, hid,
Sought its redress, release – too hard to bear

To be encased so, bandaged to be rid
Of and disposed. What was it he had done?
And where was his wife, the woman he'd wed

Whom I had seen outside their front garden,
Pruning such amaranths as live forever,
As I supposed, and her, new Eve, its warden? $_{90}$

But Peter, surely, heard us then, but never
Lifted his eyes to greet new company;
Instead, preoccupied in his own fever

Of counting: slips of paper, one... how many?
Who knew but he who reckoned, and for what?
If he could tally right, then he'd have plenty?

Yet all the while as he just shuffled, sat,
The muffling, mixed with a scratching's sound
Increased, as if behind some giant rat

Would not lie down decently dead of wounds; 100
Instead, craved life once more and all its riot,
No metal box could stop or keep her bound,

And no ignoring too would make her quiet.
So what could Peter do, or hope to do?
If she would disappear then he'd inherit

Four hundred thousand! But how make it so?
I saw him then, stopping the devil count,
Resolving, fists clenched, to have a go –

Why not? What lose, if lost in debt, debts mount?
And hell – what did he care for her, for life? 110
He said himself: she's just another cunt.

The paper slips – the sums made up his wife -
Now fluttered in the breezeless air, propelled
By static rubbed from off his skin, as if

Blades freed from the soul – dark - where they indwelled.
Some spilled into the alleyway to loiter,
Join all the shit he'd made his life, and filled;

But most, the others, like magnetic pointers,
Turned to the boot, as one cut through the lock,
Revealing whose pain occupied its centre: 120

There, there – her finger stretched, itself in shock,
Trembling with degrees no earthly nail could –
Demanding air around him be his dock

And judge according to all that was good,
For would not pure air know it? In his hand
His hammer raised to crush her at her root,

Remove all trace, pulverise to the ground.
How he glowed then, a traffic light gone red,
Bright red. As if beyond money, he'd found

What he'd always wanted: to kill the dead ₁₃₀
Beyond any chance they'd return or heal.
So now as hammer hovered, about to speed,

Then Li let forth her scream, primal and shrill,
As one soprano might who shatters glass,
Despite how hard the glass or set its will

To not break down, so now Peter, aghast,
Involuntarily stupefied, stepped
Back, and not only him – the vocal blast

Amazed Dante, who though Paradise-prepped,
Inured as it were to all our suffering, ₁₄₀
Suddenly felt again the mortal depths

From which heaven itself had been his buffering,
Till now. And I, I could not bear the pain,
The voice, the broken heart and its offering;

Thinking obliterated in the strain
Of hearing her hurt that would never still.
'Stop, stop,' I stammered, rambling and in vain,

For I fell resistless, bereft of will
And more (such was her sound) desire to live.
How long suspended in that state of nil, ₁₅₀

Who knows? Only at last there came reprieve
As Dante raised me and her cry was gone.
At last, then, my chance to strengthen, revive,

But as I mounted, limbs felt like they were stone
Which I could barely flex or mobilise.
I wanted so much to see what was done;

My body could not turn, only my eyes
Swivelled in their sockets, popping to see
This killer who'd married and vowed with lies -

65

For marriage on marriage means bigamy - $_{160}$
Alongside the murder now on his hands.
Had he - ever - one shred of care for Li?

My neck clicked sharp, as some vertebral strand
Snapped back into place, so I began thawing
With pity even, it seemed, for the damned

Here before me, horrors always gnawing
Deep, deep into being, and their dead souls;
Released, I turned now to witness their warring:

To find him smouldering like some burnt-out coal
Which even as its surface cools and ashes form, $_{170}$
Its hot interior still from its central pole

Continues threshing heat and toxic storms
Towards her whom he'd sworn to love, protect;
And she, freed now from the boot, free to swarm

All over him who'd also sold her sex,
Pimped her at parties, not regarding woman,
The divine feminine, its power to hex

The male and subtract all that is human:
Now, now she did – her voice had paralysed
Through its high-pitch the power of this conman, $_{180}$

But now attentive – his heat neutralised –
And arched beside his burning ear she perched,
Not bird-like, but as bees, billion-eyed

And buzzing low, so almost scarcely heard,
But faintly now what I had not before,
The hum was clear, but not for me her words.

These only he could hear, some music score
Written by madness to the orbit of
His brain – I saw him - flinch, as if at core –

His eye - some bee stung, stinging not enough, *190*
Dying, another took its place to sting.
How he raged then, each prick so fine, yet rough

As poison like sandpaper scraping in,
Only as liquid, free to flow and scrub
His surfaces, and strip his very being.

Her high notes first to penetrate and probe,
Freeze all his burning, remit his heat back
So he himself could feel his own heat's rub;

Then buzzing - deep, sticky - keeping him stuck
To suffering he'd made. How his colour changed *200*
And changed again, from red to white to black,

As all her sounds he writhed to have expunged;
To enter silence, oh! for him real good -
If but his soul might be immersed, be plunged,

Into the stillness of a vacant wood
Where cosmic nothings flit in shadow shapes;
No sound, no light, nor even moral should

Upsets their vagaries or killing japes;
Where cursing One who never was or is
Provokes no payback, or endless mishap, *210*

Then that, not this, would be eternal bliss;
If only. And still I saw him wrestle with fate,
Attempt to own it, make it wholly his,

But always in the din I heard 'too late' -
Some last vestige of lost meaning, noise had
To strain to whisper and articulate.

Before my eyes, he seemed to be unmade,
As moment by moment his colour dimmed
And all his vital strength began to fade;

But his contagion invited me in. *220*
A kind of panic overwhelmed me now;
Existence once so full through him waned thin.

He'd been no sun but moon, and moons too glow,
But even that light seemed crippled and weak;
And in its faltering and just overthrow

I felt a fascination with the bleak
And fatal, which held me to my own shame;
For rather than move to that which I seek

I stood there stupefied, until my name,
Suddenly in one sharp and savage bark *230*
Broke through my fog, exposing the grim game

Betraying souls to loiter in their dark.
Dante had called, and his expression held
No warmth, but rather a contempt so sharp

I knew how he'd been moved to sense the world
Again, absent so long in paradise.
His hand into my shoulder, a rough meld,

Forced me forward to some alternative
Where I might revel in some deeper vice.

CANTO 9: MASS MURDERER

The **Argument:**
  The Poet, fascinated by the destruction of his murdering neighbour, is chastised by Dante, and forced forward to encounter a deeper level of murder: one impelled by political necessity and decision-making. Here not only the murders are repellent, but the self-justifications that go along with them. Being 'sincere' and 'sincerely believing' prove convenient covers for those wishing to perpetrate evil, and without any real remorse. Bliar is finally pulled down by his victims.

> *I do not know how long that tunnel was*
> *Down which I went, escaping Peter's rage*
> *That burnt so impotently, but no pause*
>
> *In Dante's rush allowed me time to gauge*
> *Exactly what happened, or what events*
> *I might have seen at each damnation's stage;*
>
> *How many levels missed, then, as hell bent*
> *Downwards and lower, in some colony*
> *Where each shade busied itself like some ant*

Might? And, like ants, the sense of acts not free [10]
Because here genes irreversibly changed,
Trapped in enacting their own felony

Forever. Now I knew: nothing expunged
The crimes, and knowing brought its special grief -
Family, friends, neighbours, all lost, arraigned

Before the bar of their obsessive briefs
Which now they came to full possession of;
Their portion, part, to always live in death,

Unleashed from flesh, then from the source of love.
How wearisome indeed, I could scarce stand [20]
To think, much less to feel its dread enough

And know some punishment, some mighty hand
Subjected all those living to its Will;
And here nothing against could countermand

That Will that wrought enmity to all ill;
That would not countenance one twist of wrong,
Or deviation to the way of evil.

Miriam sang, long ago, her new song,
Recalling how in the surging Red Sea
What seemed impossible that hand had won [30]

And all of Pharaoh's had come not to be.
With one rebuke the whole Sea dried at root;
Through depths exposed at last to scrutiny,

A people touching soil before no foot
Had felt – what release for it: no tons of water
Pressed, merely the slight weight of human noughts:

Those vanishing - every son, every daughter -
On canvasses that time's destruction brings
In whirligigs and wildernesses later.

For each one, yes, against their own soul sins, *40*
As Dathan, Korah and Abiram found,
Like scorpions perishing from their own stings;

Only unlike such piercings was the ground
As Moses summoned the people stand back,
And all the earth where Korah was, and sand

Around his tents shifted to void and slack
And down they went, still living ... for a while ...
Till covered and lost in a soundless black.

A moment people stood, as on a hill
Beside their leader, Moses, safe by him, *50*
As all the others, in an instant, fell

To darkness; then the dread of Him on them
Broke out like plague - some mad infection spread
Faster than light, or faster than a dream

Of comfort turns to nightmare, though in bed.
So Israel's tribes bolted every which way,
Not trusting Him, for fear they too be dead.

I saw with my own eyes those damned that day
And wondered what it presaged, and where now
These wards of hell would force my sight to stray. *60*

Only, beside, Dante, I knew would know;
To him then turning, whose face I'd not seen
Since that high scream his being discomposed

And rattled, even though a son of heaven,
And he to me so sharp in his contempt,
As if the deathless life that he'd been given

Reversed – a fortune had and now all spent.
Who there to blame, as humans do, but me?
Despite my pain and fear - never absent -

71

Yet here some fellow feeling rose for Dante, *70*
Which as immortal I'd not felt before;
And so, because I felt for him such pity,

With confidence I raised my eyes and saw
Him now, ahead of my actions: his gaze,
Serene, secure, and focused in my core,

Undimmed; indeed, some greater power blazed
Within him, proof – his flame, steady from without,
Internally furious - that evil raised

Only the greater consequence of good
And in the suffering centre, that Will laughed; *80*
For nothing turned its purpose, caused it doubt.

Thus words almost seemed useless here, pure chaff,
But Dante knew it and knew all my heart.
He was himself now, and more than enough;

All loss restored, and the power of his art.
'Bless you,' he said, 'Forgive that lapse I had
When at that sound once more the human hurt

Pierced through the spirit realms with all its bad,
And stirred remembrances that heaven purged
When I cast off my flesh and was remade. *90*

But that Will who sent me here to you, urged
That I protect and lead you on this way,
Yet doing so knew I'd feel - like you - scourged.

We enter soon a ward where we must stay
Awhile for you to count the corpses stacked
By those who wield no sword, but whose words slay

In casual purposes which they have racked
Up numberless in superb disregard
Of what is good – through them goodness is fucked,

And through them, too, all truth and beauty's barred; *100*
For self-distorting mirrors mince their mind,
So wholeness isn't ever grasped, but shards;

And like Narcissus looking, they look blind.'
His captivating words held me spell-bound
And curious also as to what I'd find

In this new ward. I barely noticed ground
We'd covered in the interim of talk,
Till there we were – a cavern vast, profound

Arched over us, of such enormous bulk -
Unlike the wards before which now seemed small -*110*
Rough-hewn, yet lodge for famous catafalques

Of those whose own big trumpets blared it all:
I saw him first, the Bliar – 'Phoney Tone' -
Grinning and gawping, yet serious too, cool?

He thought so, sure, being Britannia's own.
But something strange about his words I'd hear
Yet not detect, as muffled, like some phone

In which reverberations interfere:
The words one hears, or thinks one has, repeat,
Repeat till what should be so isn't clear. *120*

I heard him say, maybe boast, 'No defeat:
Labour with me, and three elections, not
Like this buffoon who squandered my estate.'

Behind him, some contorted toad, sad and squat,
Mouthed bubbles of clichés that floated, burst
Instantly, liquidation their just lot;

For substance, wholly absent from the first,
Never was there, not since 1917
When Lenin worked his magic - Russia cursed -

And one whole country became one gangrene. *130*
But still the jargon, and socialist 'woke',
Poured forth as if thinking had never been,

Or tolls of murders had not been uncloaked,
As if ... but there I saw him, his blank face,
His eyes fish-dead, 'equality', he croaked.

But Bliar, at least, had some semblance of grace:
Whilst Korbutt aped Nimrod, gibbering on,
The Tone welcomed us, for here was his place:

Temple, memorial to what he'd done;
I sensed the shame he felt - Korbutt beside - *140*
As if being two diminished his one;

His voice, though, the weapon he exercised
With all that rhetoric for which renowned:
Its quiver, pause, retreat, final high tide

Rushed over us, almost so that we drowned
In his rich sop of words that, as I say,
Echoed in doubled froth, doubled rebound,

Though I sensed too conflict as to which way
He'd make address to us; for on one hand
Dante he knew and how great in his day; *150*

But Dante would write no more, he understood,
Where I, perchance, though lesser far, not fit
To stand beside, yet lived in Bliar's land -

Knew of Iraq, and so might write of it
In such a style as favoured his design -
Make him look good for all the killing shit:

Four wars he entered, justified his crimes
By arguing things were far worse otherwise;
Saddam unchecked? That monster's paradigm

Of tyranny and all its murderous lies? *160*
Some half a million dead didn't compare
To all who had or would by Saddam die;

And anyway, the WMDs stored there
Meant Bliar's moral right was strong, compelling;
He said so now, and he said so, sincere.

And how sincere - that trump was his high calling!
No guilt or blood, or so he thought, attached
To one who acted sincerely in felling

Some half a million. Like – if going back
We think of Arjuna, hesitating in *170*
The chariot when god Krishna urged attack;

For Arjuna's destiny had to be won
By death, destruction, and a victory
Decisive through annihilating kin.

How Bliar beamed his smile, triumphantly,
Positioning himself beyond reproach,
And blocking Korbutt whom we couldn't see,

Though still there, furtive even as he mooched,
Sullen in ramblings of his deranged mind;
But Bliar certain he could not be touched. *180*

Away in the distance, and far behind
I heard such screams as wonder turned to fear,
And fear in turn gave way to horror's sign;

At which the ribbits faded, as never here,
For Korbutt sunk into his own foul pond,
Whilst Bliar's smile wavered to disappear;

For deep within he knew something beyond
The narcissistic echoes of his views
With all their self-congratulatory bland.

'Sincerely!' screeched – the word - so loudly through ₁₉₀
This concourse of the damned, as no surprise
But shocking all the same, and to accuse

Purveyors of its truth, which meant its lies:
There, there, in something like swirling black holes,
Which Bliar understood full well – his eyes

Reeled back into their sockets as his soul
Struggled to free itself from his own mind;
But blackness – that bright tar – gravity's pull

Began to exercise its force and bind.
I felt myself also carried to it, ₂₀₀
Like at my back irresistible wind

Blew, so that I, in that blackness, would forfeit
My Self. But Dante then reached out his arm -
Unmoved himself - he held and stopped my slip.

But Bliar had no such luck, friend or charm.
His face had drained of all blood, now sheer white
With fear, and aged with lines of lying's harm.

I'd moved an inch and saw the black so bright
Because it burned existence at its core,
Then feeding off its melt - the trapped-in light -₂₁₀

So nothing living fled its one-way door.
Light blackened as it touched its surface, lost,
And scorching the while darkness screamed for more

No matter what was destroyed, how steep the cost;
But if not light could escape, at least sound's
Agony, baking in its basted roast

Emerged in beats of pulverising wounds
Across the void in pulses that replaced
Heart beats. Instead, there where senses – spellbound -

Gripped reality's superficial face, 220
I saw their arms drag down the bleeding masks
Which one by one succeeded in that place.

A moment only, they cried out - their task –
Screaming, 'Sincerely', before the murdered arms
Re-took their thin veneers - like snake-skin husks

Of being - and pressed down till they lost form,
Or almost – for some kernel yet remained,
Which was a given, could not be returned;

And as I looked I saw their human names:
Osama Bin Laden trying to cope 230
With all the death he'd caused, and all the pain;

Dead arms had him, and in them was no hope
And no escape, as they clawed his spirit
If not to nullify, then essence rape

Beyond recovery or thought of it.
Then Hitler, too, who also loved 'sincerely',
Appeared – Osama having done his bit

Dropped down, though raging, as if he'd unfairly
Been treated - as this bigger boaster now
Emerged, and a million times more arms squarely 240

Moved up and grasped him, unfazed, un-kowtowed
By force, abuse, charismatic tirades:
They would ensure that what he'd done, he'd know.

As Bliar would – for all the deals he'd made –
For all felicities spoken, enjoined,
And promises, like Hitler's, all gone bad

Or mad – now the worth of all he'd coined
In this black furnace reached its residue
As half a million Iraqis' death he'd spawned

Now rose to draw him down to pay his dues. 250
The image of his face now topped the hole
Into the black fire, as Hitler's withdrew,

'Sincerely,' too, he screamed, as his lost soul
Attempted one last time to justify
His actions, consequences, rigmarole.

About to tip and go again to die,
And never re-emerge, so that I called
Out, 'Wait! You need to tell me, Tony, why?'

His word 'sincere' froze then, as if it palled
Beside his name spoken by one still living; 260
Who knows, could such a one have his fate stalled?

Slowly, as if to answer broke his grieving
With which he was now wholly preoccupied,
I sensed his soul and mind were locked in striving;

And one sought truth, but stronger still, he lied -
Repressing back to black eternal shining,
His mind held down the truth which it denied;

He searched for words that upheld his defining
Interpretation of what he'd achieved –
The high and moral platforms he was running; 270

But always image and never the deed.
'Here's who I am,' he said, 'Suffering, you see,
And to me it's pointless, for there's no need;

I've always said that talking sensibly
And reason's best, for which I'm optimistic;
The POTUS thought me the man of destiny;

Shoulder to shoulder, hell to all the critics –
The Cabinet, Parliament, ignore the law
And what do people know – fickle, they switch?

My mask won't slide; I know what power's for: 280
To fight all evil in the world, prevail ...'
And now he raged and would have said much more,

But fighting evil in himself had failed:
The arms had him, so down he shot to hell.

CANTO 10: BREXIT

The Argument:
   After escaping from Bliar, trapped in Canto 9 because of Iraq, the Poet is first refreshed by Dante who allows him a momentary access to the reality he enjoys. Then, the Poet encounters the European Federalists and Anti-Brexiteers in their special Ward of Hell. It starts with Napoleon and the succession of fascists who have strived to control Europe, but this leads onto even the Brits who have betrayed their people and their country, manufacturing false, specious and well-sounding arguments to overturn democracy itself.

So almost before I could realise
What happened, Bliar dropped into black heat;
And the arms holding him to cauterise

His shadow - and hope to slay his soul's seat
If but the universe permitted such –
Drew down as others rose swiftly to meet

The surface for a moment where their blotch
Of being stained the nimbus of the dark
Which, for all their screams, held them in its clutch.

Of Bliar? No trace, not even a mark $_{10}$
Was left where just before he seemed to speak;
This realisation, brutal and stark,

Served only to drain me further; so weak,
I turned exhausted and totally wretched
To where my guide, who'd been there for my sake,

Stood solid, godlike, with his arms outstretched,
And into their comfort I propelled myself,
Aching to feel existence unattached

To horrors here as was this fading gulf.
And thinking so, as my whole weight went slump $_{20}$
Against my teacher, I found his soul's stern proof

Could hold me up, and its energy jump-
Started my body with a vital power –
As null and dull myself, and he the lamp

Whose lighting charged and which no time devoured,
Diminished, circumscribed in any way;
For in one second I saw all the hours

Compressed into a zodiac of sky,
And then a thimble for a humble thumb;
And I caught – breathless – and how can I say? - $_{30}$

Some figureless form that made my mind numb
Instantly; then my spirit and soul, awe-
Struck, cried out, but in words completely dumb

Reaching across the arc of nothing for ...
What had I seen? 'Tell me,' I murmured, hoarse,
Depending on the great poet, my mentor.

'Rest now on me,' he said, 'and save your voice.
I know your thoughts and what you wish to know:
With all this misery, where is heaven's course?

How far is it that we still have to go?' 40
As words failed me, I nodded in assent;
Then something like breathing began to flow

From Dante out to me, and as it went
It seemed that I and Dante became one,
That we were joined, our spirits somehow blent;

What Dante saw, was now what I looked on:
Before, at some impossible height, a door
That we might reach at last and all be done –

And as it opened suddenly its glare
Of light flashed, blinding me - already mute - 50
But now my mortal eyes could not endure

The sight. So speechless, blind, I felt his feet
Move forward into that light where mass
Evaporated; and instead a beat

Began, all depth, a tuning fork in bass
At which vibration what was is entrained,
And will be too aligns in its light space.

Sightless, yet feeling through Dante's brain,
A flood of joy, strong as Niagara Falls,
Drenched through me, flushing out all sense of pain; 60

The more it rushed, the less that I felt full,
The more capacity I seemed to have;
And other sounds began, notes and a call,

Which whispered, as remote - as from a cave -
My name, but not the name I knew myself –
A name unknown, yet one my being craves.

As I heard it, my eyes, as if by stealth
Stole in the light and I began to see;
Slowly at first, they returning to health

And seeing but not our reality: $_{70}$
For one instant I saw who loved me, in-
filled with such faultless light, all visionary;

A holy company of women and men
Awaiting me - and round their heads, rainbows
Of colours beyond the earth's narrow span,

And in their very living, all life glowed.
They looked on me as one who was their child,
Forever theirs to love, and be it so.

I gasped for breath, and once more sought to hold
My Dante – overwhelmed by beauty there – $_{80}$
Too conscious my presence somehow defiled

That holy place – so holy, and somewhere
I should not, could not be. And with that thought
Dante's footsteps went into a reverse,

And backwards stumbling, losing what I'd caught,
I heard the door click shut, and me bereft
Of such a love abruptly now cut short.

So heaven itself seemed subject to theft:
The Maker of all had an empty hand,
And all life's glory finally was less $_{90}$

And lost? To loiter here, then, with the damned?
I looked around: one road back to black heat,
And one ahead, to deeper desolate lands?

What did this mean, and how escape this pit?
Now Dante took my hand and simply said,
'Be still your soul – your destiny's to meet

Again – and twice – those above who're dead,
But live forever through Him who broke through
These evil corridors - Him whom death dreads.

There is a mansion, be sure, and for you 100
They wait, as you saw, before your doubt reared
Its head. Now let's go – there's further below.'

And as I scanned his face, I thought a tear
Ran down his cheeks, immortal though they shone:
Had he succumbed to all the sickness here?

But then I realised that I was wrong:
Transported back to heaven as we had
For those few moments reproduced its song

In Dante, who now untouched by any bad,
Could not but feel the joy to which returning 110
Here made contrast, because here all was shade

Or else was lost in tinder of its burning;
But just the knowing heaven is above
Forever, always, how could not his yearning

Soul not respond in feeling of that love?
I choked myself as this awareness struck,
And to disguise, quickly began to move.

But with celestial spirits no such luck:
For Dante knew, as his tear quite transformed
Itself; and what was sorrow's engraved track 120

Now seemed a diamond - though rough carbon-wombed -
With all the brilliance, clarity too,
Of something, simply, immortally born.

I need say nothing now, for he just knew –
His diamond like a lens absorbing light
Which at the same time showed me through and through

And to myself therefore, still lost in night.
But moving forward meant repentance wait,
For soon enough we'd be at our next plight.

I felt the air menace with more than hate; *130*
Some deeper level of evil, more cold
And calculating its approaching fate:

Ahead, an architecture, striking, bold,
Symbolic of one who living had sought
To build colossal unity which held

Europe infected - a virus caught
Through violence, swathes of levelling law
By which mankind's deceived and all's sold short.

Equality, brotherhood, the cause
And liberty too – they to outdo God *140*
In goodness human, secular in source;

And there he was, bicorn cocked at an odd
Angle, and on an island all his own;
Except a shadow, sleuthing, glowing red,

As if some twin who shared a common name;
With above him stone, monumental, carved,
Proclaiming forever his brutal shame:

A mouth opening for the shadow it served,
Wailing, 'Napoleon, Europe expects –
Return – finish the task from which you swerved'. *150*

An omen then, a god in that stone tract,
But not Athena, no; I'd no idea
So turned to Dante, puzzled, perplexed –

His finger pointing, mind already there.
'Now watch,' he said, 'and see the only devil
This emperor worships. You know him, Ares.'

I gasped. And saw redden further, and spiral
Right round Napoleon's form and through his heart
The one who stirred those vicious to more evil;

How Boney shook, as fit to fall apart, ₁₆₀
The while in low and guttural tones, and reddening
Further and deeper as he probed to hurt

Boney, his agent, voice always threatening,
Till Boney, held unbearable in suspense,
At last let loose his scream with its deadening

Precision. Only Dante never winced;
I ducked, as if some missile shot my way,
Which, if it touched, I'd die – follow, convinced.

My mind would lose itself, as a dog strays
And finally finds ten thousand marching men ₁₇₀
All bent on virtue, and each dog his day;

The women too, but no time to see them;
His cursed cry led one carnage to the next -
I saw the Kaiser, lost in futile dreams,

His withered arm, his soul, of no effect,
As grasping Europa, still she escaped.
Beyond them all, though, one whose cruel lex

Extended from France to Russia's rape;
Now in a bunker where Berlin breaks down
Into fragments, mosaics of a shape; ₁₈₀

And so Adolf, who'd once worn Europe's crown,
Now seemed – blasted into blown smithereens,
Which held his semblance, figured in dead bones.

They had in common - all these hateful has-beens -
One book in which their dream was written large:
Ares, the author of these destructive scenes,

That from his very loins all poison urged
Europa fall, be taken, overwhelmed
By one dictator whose semen surged

Till at the topmost point of time's packed helm 190
There'd be the loyal lieutenant, Are's man,
All Europe his, and all Europe one realm.

But violence, exhausted, no longer spanned
The continent. Others had their work to do;
I looked and saw their faces, what they planned:

Preachers of peace who in the darkness glowed
With deeper angers than even Hitler had;
Awaiting time when for their god they'd show

Their faces' true aspect in all its mad.
There was the man – who when it's serious, lies –200
Determined to bury Britain with his spade;

Beside him, Tisk, who busy swallowing pieces
Of vomit, morsels baked brown in his own guts,
Regurgitated them – and with loose faeces

They loved - like longing lovers (Buncker, he) - put,
Sickening, through their own beings. In the gloom
The nausea even kept Boney's eyes shut.

And more: The English traitors in the room.
I saw them – Swindle, Minor, Bezzletine;
Her primping herself with Brussels' perfume 210

Like some sow thinking ditch water white wine,
Intoxicated by bacteria drunk;
The memes, acorns, clichés, high pitched whine,

Till like a full fed hog sat clueless, and stank.
As Minor huffed and puffed 'considered opinions',
Which paltry phrase just made his views more rank

And odious – which he knew, as one with onions
Under his eyes, must weep and weep, without
Reserve because nothing he'd done was done:

All half-truths, evasions, get-outs, and buts; 220
Pure compromises, equivocations, deals
With one design: to keep the British shut

Down in a place where nothing, no-one heals.
'Where are we?' I cried out. 'What is this place?'
Minor's greyed eyes lifted like two jellied eels:

And jellied tears congealing, stuck to his face
In hideous caricature of real grief.
Answering, weakly, and with no trace

Of true commitment, authentic belief,
He said, 'In my considered view ...' and then 230
His voice dropped off, as from a tree a leaf

Floats free, and vaguely drifts into the wind.
So Minor now could make no sense of it;
Europe had addled his wits, destroyed his mind;

Just darkness left, and sitting, eating shit.
Then Dante interposed to clarify:
'All hospitals have beneath them deeper pits

Where hot incinerators burn and try
To rid the souls of their infectious fevers,
But none of these so self-important 'I's 240

Can ever be free. For them heaven is never
Available. Like Arachne with her webs,
Thinking to outwit the goddess as a weaver,

So they rage with stories, seemingly with legs,
Until at last caught out (compete with wisdom?
Who would who's sane?) they fade as power ebbs

In death and that eternal law holds them;
Forever spinning, but all pointless Babels,
Building no living fabric, but a tomb

In which all that is human is disabled. ₂₅₀
I felt a roaring heat ahead, approaching,
That would consume all 'woken', self-labelled

And virtue-signalling hypocrites, all cringing
As fire that washes them to finer grey
Advanced. 'We must be gone. No time for lingering,'

Said Dante. 'Your body will burn like hay.'
But Bezzletine suddenly, a dying owl,
Hooted his final threat, to earn his pay:

'Cowards and racists all, little England's foul...'
His mace - his arm could barely wield - fell back – ₂₆₀
wards, puncturing his chest, whilst splitting his soul.

So there he lay, exposed, on the fire's track,
Which now almost upon us, its heat singed
My hair – and at my body its first flak

Surged. 'Leap,' dear Dante shrieked – and so I jumped,
And just in time. Behind, the second wave
Fried every soul whom Europe had unhinged.

But falling where I did, one still alive
I heard rebuking punishment, insisting
On 'Order, Order'. I turned in the cave ₂₇₀

Into which I'd fallen to see resisting
A thousand-year destiny, the British will,
One evil, pock-faced toad, great at oppressing

All brethren - women too, fated to sit still
And suffer his commands – such was Barquo,
A traitor suited, fitted for such ill.

But even he – what really did he know?
This heat unleashed, no spell of his could stop;
Indeed, he gasped in agony, all a-glow,

And turning grey - not even green to rot - 280
His powdered form flaked down to its job lot.

CANTO 11: POETASTERS

The **Argument:**
The Poet, having escaped the HellWard of European dicta-tors and corrupt British politicians, emerges into the penulti-mate HellWard depth where he, with his guide, Dante, meets the Poetasters from America and Britain. These lost souls have denied Apollo and the real meaning and purpose of poetry. They have, thus, have been guilty of promoting a most heinous crime and so must finally encounter the River Lethe.

> As Barquo found himself reduced to ash,
> And I looked on, astonished by his fate -
> How easily the self-important crash;
>
> It seemed there is One whose patience can wait
> Till just that moment when some reach their peak
> Of evil, and then destruction looms – too late,
>
> Another way's not there, not what they seek:
> Too long the training in perversity
> For souls who love the darkness, laud the bleak.

But I was now somewhere constricting me: *10*
A cave and entrance, slanting to a ward
Existing lower, with weird symmetry

Ahead. However, still I had my guard -
My master - Dante, whose hands dragged me forth
Until I saw the cave led to the mad,

The truly mad. This ward, full of such worth-
less individuals, claiming Apollo theirs;
And on each other's heads, they placed the wreaths

Of laurel, as pretending they had shares
In Daphne's victory, the evergreen *20*
Apollo made, for true poets to wear.

Here even Dante wearied at the scene,
As if the heaven he was in could not
Protect him from writings, low and obscene.

To see such scribblings, such vagaries, blots,
More like graffiti than serious works,
Defacing truth, the while their authors gloat

As simians might whose fingers at nits pick;
Or primates in their hierarchies might
Preen themselves – keen on set-ups for their perks! *30*

A sudden Howl ahead shook me with fright
As via the pointless air it blasted through,
Much as a tunnel is with dynamite;

But this was different and this was new –
At least a tunnel had a purpose, led
From one obstruction to a better view;

But this was pure calamity, and fed
On energy that had a darker take;
Conceived entirely not from soul, but head;

Fools thinking Apollo fooled, while they, ego-wracked, 40
Devised false words to undermine true meaning;
Theirs a license – to break rules, free their snake

Whose mantra hisses 'freedom', its scales gleaming,
But freedom's far from brotherhoods they preach,
And those confusions which their failed explainings

Never explain - or poetry could reach.
For now, we came closer to the sound's source –
Which much resembled a muddy, filthy ditch;

So little light and even less remorse
As one small man attempted to leap out 50
From the pitch that held him, but, lacking force,

His efforts sunk him back whilst still afloat.
He saw me, then, and howled anew, 'Hey, you,
The weight of the world is love; this isn't rot –

Never forget you don't know till you do.
Help me escape this awful pit, and see
Sweet Kaddish, hey, my inner moonlight through'.

But at this Dante moved in front of me,
And gestured with a sign that seemed to stir
The mud, so it rotated, at first slowly, 60

As some laxed bit a knackered horse might spur
To pick up speed; and as it did, the lines
Within the mud began to form, emerge

With their distinctive feature: no design
At all! And Jinnsberg, excited the while,
Whooped wildly, hands splayed out, 'This is all mine,'

Though speaking, words distorted to a howl,
I not sure then, did he say, 'mine' or 'mean',
Or even was it 'men', his vowels, foul

And slippery, pure outages of his spleen, 70
Could not control his consonantal phrasing:
Instead of meaning, sound became a stain

That blotched the air, insisting on self-praising -
As if superb merit inhered in glug,
Or debasing language was itself pleasing.

But Dante, conjuring the ditch - now like a jug -
Whose contents whirled in the mud-storm that spun
Forcing Jinnsberg down, as water in a plug –

I saw those gimlet eyes, knowing their con
About to be exposed, his lifeline cut, 80
And only endless dirt to bite, chew on.

His fear, hysterical as a boil sealed shut
Beneath the skin, but bursting to explode,
Yet downwards forced as Jinnsberg surged up

One time more; and his works – 'Madness: An Ode' –
Now like himself dragged down to where no eye
Could see such a detour from the right road,

Or plumb its depth – can madness satisfy?
But even as, finally, he disappeared -
With all the counterculture and its lies - 90

Where falsehood suffers, is no longer cheered
By all the rabble worshipping its shit-jelly,
So at that point another noise I heard:

Raphael mai amech izabi almi,
Repeated, bellow-like, a stuck refrain;
Then seeing one - sized like a redwood tree -

Gigantic, huge, but captured here in chains
Which fixed him from waist down into the earth;
Also, held arms strapped to his heart in pain,

As if gainsaid desire to vaunt his worth $_{100}$
In words, which now he never would be able
To do. 'Behold,' said Dante, 'Nimrod's curse –

The cause of more than war, something too subtle:
Confusing all the languages of the world,
Rendering Adam's poetry fitful babble,

As now you hear with Jinnsberg and his fold.
Indeed, you've more to hear before we're done.'
He paused – I thought, a moment, looking old.

While Nimrod raged, he murmured to me, 'Son,
I hoped to never see these giants more; $_{110}$
But for your sake I do. Let's now press on.'

Which glad I was – the rage at Nimrod's core
Seemed strong enough to break even his bonds,
Though forged in heaven, so safely secure.

'Tell me', I said, as we marched this queer land
Of strange perspectives, deadening artefacts,
And gnostic nonsense no-one understood –

'How is it poets suffer at this depth?
Why, then, this ward especially for them,
Below the dross of EU Federalists?' $_{120}$

'First, son,' he said, 'be clear: not from the stem
Of laurel tended by Apollo do
These weeds emerge, infesting all that's clean

And wholesome with linguistic dribble, spew;
Concoctions of venom, deep in their souls,
Produce old poisons, though revamped as new;

Forgetting, holy Psalmist, and the fool
Who says in his false heart, there is no God;
So godless, they must go to nothing's hole

Where now you see them sinking; though they bob 130
Awhile, their manic energies consumed,
Last flickering of ego before it's dropped

And in themselves they're thoroughly entombed.
Why, here's a famous poet wannabe,
Who pilfered laurels on his frantic climb

To be America's biggest me, me, me!'
I looked and saw Wilt Witless yawping hard
With sounds barbaric and untranslatably

Full, singing self with multitudes of words.'
How pitiful he seemed, jaw in a lock, 140
Noise foaming forth, as spittle flew like birds

In sprays before his mouth which couldn't stop
Its own inelegance from sounding trash.
As Jinnsberg sank, so Witless now was topped

By spit – his own reflux - turning to ash
All verses his deranged mind baptized art;
He himself pulverised in dirt's dire crush.

Yet like Nimrod, the master-mind and heart
Of this cruel caprice leading nowhere,
So Witless in his pride was set apart. 150

Nothing that any said, any could bear -
Though living, citing names for lineage,
Was practice, necessary, de rigueur -

But each hated the other with furious rage;
And more, despised true poets writing true,
Inspired by beauty, goodness and what's sage.

Part of their sentence, then, was hid from view:
Their splutter, like some hornet taking flight,
Alighted in their ears and stung them through –

Right through, to deafen first, then deaden right 160
By piercing up towards their addled brains:
So deaf they struggled, in their pickled plight;

The while their own malice surged through their veins.
Ultimately, all coherence would be lost,
Except a tiny soul, bleating, insane,

Bequeathing, as Witless did, vapid boasts
Of self-promotion impressing no-one;
For powerless as leaves on water float,

So they all struggled, and would still, till done.
But Dante, I knew, could barely stand it; 170
Knowing Apollo, the laurels he'd won -

Though he might, and could in one instance flit
To heaven - I sensed deep discomfiture,
So tried to turn him. 'What about the Brits?

American poets – these - damned for sure;
But on the other side where England is,
Do poets there provide the classic cure?'

Mark Dante then – almost in hysterics!
When laughing ceased, and he regained himself,
His mood changed, (as by my question oddly fixed), 180

'Your poets, once upon a time, had wealth –
For Shakespeare showed the way of form with feeling;
Such that the Muse herself inspired real truth,

But now –' he indicated where the ceiling
Of the ward narrowed and space seemed confined;
Where English poets dealt more damned readings -

If that were possible - than Americans bound
In all their epic and expansive poses.
There was one seated, sighing a soft sound,

Who not in pain, might be as one who dozes *190*
Quietly in Oxford chambers, dreaming spires,
With certain privileges which simply ooze

Off him - old world reticence which retires
Rather than brazen Yankee-doodle style;
But that would underestimate his fires

Which burnt as fiercely as any Witless wills;
And will's the word, for that only accounts
For all his rubbish, dry as coffee spills,

As not one Muse his soul inspires, or mounts
Parnassus; for only there is sound light; *200*
But check, real musing's not what this one wants.

Instead, and nevertheless - to climb the heights
Though talentless. Thus, he stirred and I saw
A merry gargoyle grimace – its first sleight -

Corrupt his casual face, revealing more:
'Tell Tony', he said, meaning Bliar PM,
'I really want it, add it to my score.'

The Laureateship, no question, his then!
On his terms too – as, 'Let's do a decade',
So blot four hundred years with new-spun phlegm! *210*

But wrong before: as now began to fade
That pain-free persona he had perfected;
And like a rotten wall, stripped of its façade,

Another being emerged, but defective.
The blond Adonis, Tony's blue-eyed chum,
Who starred with Auden, Larkin; so connected

This mummy's boy who knows, who goes, who comes -
To whom the English-speaking world presents
Its prizes in all of London's glittering rooms;

Now feels his own substance, like skin, absent; 220
Now his soul roiling - as in boiling water -
Wants proof, some legacy, that's cool as cement

To hold together pallid nonsense fought for
In that campaign begun so long ago.
Indeed, is he a poet? How be sure?

And how be certain he, or the world knows?
How not, like Laureates before, go down
Down, down to where chill streams of Lethe flow?

Remember – hot his collar now, and frowns
Disfigure that once perfect brow – their names? 230
Yes, Austin, Whitehead, Shadwell wore the crown,

As Pye, Bridges, Eusden, Tate, had their time;
And not forgetting those we have forgotten –
Rowe, Cibber, Masefield, Lewis – such a line;

All ones appointed by judgements gone rotten,
For whom Apollo never shone, or spoke -
Allowed the true sublime to be begotten.

The hell of it – to come round and be woke:
That is, to find such papers in his hand,
Crumbling to pieces from his ego's shock, 240

Discovering no-one cares, or understands
One stanza or one line he ever wrote –
That poets be oceans; he is a pond.

The final proof? Poetry no-one quotes.
And now insouciance freezes, alters,
A rictus fixed on the river - there notes

How many poets faked it, till they faltered
To fall in Lethe's stream of nothingness
Where in its coldest waste no sound is uttered.

I saw his larynx warble, quite muscle-less, ₂₅₀
Unable to turn a phrase, describe his torture,
Though wordsmith once - with words like trots unleashed -

But now no words available to soar.
And so the dreadful stream flowed on and on,
And he – on fire – tipped over for his cure:

Imagine it! As Lethe's surface shone
With all its frigid, fascinating foam,
Sir Handy, like a comet plunged straight down,

And as a coal in water hisses steam,
So Handy was - in his monstrous collapse - ₂₆₀
Into that flux where being's never been.

I heard, alongside the huge hissing, perhaps
One other sound, so low, inaudible
Except, I knew, as one escaping traps

Feels, and thus sighs: so deep, his source of trouble -
Now whisked away, already cooling, soon
No trace beneath the water, not one bubble

Left to proclaim he'd lived, because he'd gone
Along with his imposture, poetry too.
And I, despite myself, stood there, just stunned: ₂₇₀

That last sound, was what? My soul in me knew –
And now perhaps as Adam did for Cain,
Not Abel, felt loss from his endless rue;

The wreck of will, the chance to be again.
I cried aloud. Sir Handy would not return;
His mother's hopes – whatever – were in vain;

All might-have-beens lost, and now of hope shorn;
The river's icy grip gave no release –
For Judas also could not be reborn.

Now Dante tried to comfort, bring me peace. 280
'Your tears, my son - misplaced and do you hurt.
Sir Handy had his honour, though but leased;

Like Pharisees praying, but not from their hearts;
They had their honours that they sought from men,
Whilst they ignored Him, he the Muses' arts.

Compassion elevates the human mien,
But pity here is pointless and askew ...'
I longed once more to see Apollo's sun,

To see it shine where honeysuckle grew,
And turn to find the Muses by my side 290
Laughing with joy, and prompting me anew

To hear the song that Orpheus strummed and played.
Not this, not Lethe and its tuneless cold,
But still our exit my master delayed,

Pointing, as we quit the friendless fold,
Another edging towards the dark brink,
Who babbled on about her poetry sold;

Proudly, first Scot, first woman, and first dyke;
It's all big history now with Laureateship –
And for the people, which is what they like! 300

I wanted to stay, see her verses slip
But Dante reprimanded me – 'It's gross,'
He said, 'Enjoying that she writes pure shit'.

With that, what answer sufficed? At a loss -
My contradiction pity lately led -
I turned away: to be a poet cost.

Perhaps here, I too, became as bad;
Instead of curses it was time to bless,
For only blessings let poetry be made.

Closer she drew to the brink's black abyss, 310
Like some white queen, who skipping in her pride,
Thinks - King abandoned - sharp moves win her chess.

I tried to help - shout across our divide;
But near those waters even my words died.

CANTO 12: PHILOSOPHERS

The **Argument:**
 The Poet, having escaped the HellWard of false prophets and poetasters now encounters the false philosophers whose ideas have spread misery and mayhem to so many. One whose song epitomises all the false promises of secularism; another who has led women to deny themselves and their nature; and finally, Satan's final trick - a populist and scientist claiming God does not exist. But the god Apollo appears and his light shows the way out of hell.

How dire contamination is: if language
Proves false, how disinfect the stench of words?
Or how restore the love that's heaven's message

For what it is - ignored, or never heard,
As down the stream of Lethe flows away
Even the very souls of would-be bards.

The colour of my own sounds now seemed grey.
I'd tried to help her, but how weak I was;
Despite my shout, her verse had gone astray,

Not knowing Apollo was not by-passed, ₁₀
Or that his daughters could not be defied.
O Man! A little while you paint your gloss

And then the deluge comes and you're surprised!
All things in Lethe's river meet their end
And only those who seek the gods survive.

Woe, and again, to them who laugh and spend
Their one and only time imagining glory:
Some victory to which their life will wend

And vindicate their choices - and their story -
Abandoning all belief in power above: ₂₀
To be in such depths where there's no word sorry,

Yet feel its absence, that absence of love
Completely. Dante sensed my grief and now
Drew close to comfort, give me what I craved -

In all this dark - that still heaven exposed
Something more precious still - all was not lost.
True, false poets on words overdosed

And were by their own lines condemned the most;
But those whom Orpheus taught to sing know well
How suffering pain must be - so pay the cost: ₃₀

How, in the depths of feeling's pit of hell,
True poets sing the song to somewhere else,
Where heaven forms, even as their words spell

It. 'Nearly there,' he said. 'The last who have no selves,
Beyond where fires incinerate their waste -
Their waste wasted — where what they were dissolves

To liquid slop, and truly being's defaced:
Their mothers would not own or recognise.
And then we climb.' He smiled. 'With haste'.

How Dante radiated love in his eyes; 40
I felt myself consoled. We walked at pace,
Down stairwells following Lethe's subtleties,

But as we went I felt lost in a maze,
Worse even than the bibble-babble past.
The furniture distorted, shapeless, crazed,

No longer fit to use, or made to last:
Ephemeral objects built only to break –
Creations finally of minds gone west.

And Dante knew my thoughts, what questions raked
My being, struggling here to comprehend 50
This ward where ovens thaw-through those half-baked!

'Be careful,' Dante said, 'for here's the end
Of hell itself in your world: the last test –
Philosophers whose ideas never mend

Or heal a single soul; rather, as pests -
Cockroaches scuttling in cellars below -
They quarry till your kitchen is their nest.

Too late, then, once inside, to bid them go –
Infesting food with filth, and puke-fed bugs
All right-thinking folk shun and disavow.' 60

He would say more, but some twangy sound drugged –
Anthemic dirge narcotising - the air.
One corpse in the corner, with four holes plugged

By bullets, sang about imagine there
Is love, no heaven, (and he said) no hell,
But peace; and all the sages joined his choir

And everything utopian would be well!
Yet as his bass played and his ditty rose,
I sensed at first what soon was a sick smell;

And I recoiled – my hand up to my nose, *70*
For there all wisdom's rot was in one song:
Whilst Omo Lemon simply decomposed –

For how could such philosophy last long?
The ward now shook, as if some earthquake might
Compound destructions that were going on –

So Lemon, melting, became walrus-like
In feature, till the notes he sang all flattened
And sound found silence as he lost all light.

No more the walrus even; for no pattern
Of what he had been remained in that ward; *80*
Author and song, all being was unwritten -

Each note unpicking his quickening chord.
'Be clear,' said Dante sternly, 'there's no hope
For those who think their efforts earn rewards:

They've only one line, and that's Judas' rope.'
I look confused. 'But surely, we all want -
Expect - our works to show our best side up?'

Deep quiet followed in breaths I could count -
Then felt a scorn more withering than before,
Which pained me with a sense of deepest taint. *90*

Now Dante turned - with such conviction sure
As heaven only powered its top pitch:
'Until you drink pure milk, there is no cure.

Strong food's no use for a malnourished wretch;
Why gobble down and not discriminate,
Only to find what you consume's too rich?

For here, truly, the food is food to hate:
Seemingly solid fare, seemingly good -
Prepared to feed you, lead you, to their fate.

This sergeant peppers, pipes, over this wood 100
With flimsy overtures to entertain;
But he's a junior of this fatal brood.

See captains, colonels with more potent strains.
Singers seduce the simpletons with tunes,
But soldiers of the intellectual brain –

I will not deign to call it mind – use runes,
Inventions, symbols of their own desires,
To mark their rank; and One Himself impugn

With failure – as if! As if their failed wares
Could substitute for the great cosmos formed 110
By Him from nothing and His heart of fire;

The One whose Word' – how majestic then – 'calmed
Chaos' own self' – Dante appeared, as if
His blazing thought had detonated qualms,

Killed doubts, exploded all their sophistry;
And, righteous in his rage, the wards of hell
Trembled, for judgement, terrible and swift,

Already worked its unbreakable will.
But now, ahead, an interruption beckoned:
A fading soul cried out, greying, female; 120

Defiant too - but here more than she reckoned
With. 'Help me', words I thought aimed at us.
But as I looked, her mist-like grey changed, blackened;

As did her language: 'You fuck,' and every cuss
Known. 'I'm repressed, and no-one is free;
Women must choose – fuck them too; they're all wuss;

But me? I am the daughter of destiny –
I've cut down men – it's easy – no right tit -
So with my bow I shot the great Achilles,

Missing! Then that hot bot got in my slit. ₁₃₀
Hell! What a weapon wielded, struck me with,
Killing me, but as he did, that was it:

We fell in love; but I was dead enough,
Only my carcass screwed man after man;
But I adored the rough of sterile stuff.'

At this she paused - to cover-up her plan
Or part thereof? But who was she? And why
Trapped here? Said Dante, 'Here's an Amazon,

Who not for sex suffers, and all the guys
Seduced – or those abortions in her bed - ₁₄₀
But rather – first - her sick philosophy.

Her ideas drew women from womanhood:
Some sister posing in her prophet's part;
Or siren wreaking havoc in their heads,

Till on the rocks of crashed and lonely hurt
She left them; while she, other fish to fry,
Practised infamy as fame's whoring tart.

Look! Her great cry is all of liberty,
Enslaved herself by every known lust,
And most of all, within, cossetting envy.' ₁₅₀

At these last words she turned, her jaw up-thrust
In proud defiance. 'You, you giant poet!
I've heard of you – so fucking you's a plus;

But Nobody there, is your cock-sucking midget?
He's nothing, no-one, never in your league,
Why bother? I'm here and real and not frigid;

You could – we could – explore my fetid fig,
Then write a canto undermining men,
Manhood, and prove – let's face it – they're all pigs'.

And suddenly, though welded to dead stone, *160*
She sprang forward, attacking - her whole frame
A projectile at Dante, aimed and thrown.

I flinched, dazed, too slow to shout his name
And warn him to avoid her vicious blow;
But he just stood there, impassive, the same,

As her clenched fist smote down with all its show
Of force – and as it did so, vaporised,
For she'd become virtually nothing now,

So even her black shade (– before my eyes –
Receded, reluctant, to that fog-grey *170*
That first I'd seen –) dematerialised,

As if into still finer drops of spray;
And so what seemed a strike was some dull cloud
That harmless, brushed his spirit, fell away.

Dante then turned, dismissive, said aloud:
'This one misled so many, many millions,
Which doing so – she held wit - made her proud;

The essence of Satan and all his minions –
To make their misery contagious, widespread,
To share their load and forge their pain in common; *180*

To out-think God, contain Him in their heads,
Disguise their jealousy with smooth veneers
Concocted in darkness, as vermin's bred.

This one, known in the world as Leia Leer,
Take your last look, and note her eunuch marks,
As every human feature disappears.'

Her soul so scrubbed with vacant, deadening works;
Her masquerades of self-promotion posing
As offerings; all seeds of that old Anarch

Allowing Satan through to mankind's losing: 190
Some pit not even Beelzebub might mine;
For therein - the void - was no life but closing.

I had to move on - running out of time;
Since if I stayed much longer in these wards -
Prolonged exposure - would their thoughts be mine?

A sense of urgency stirred me onwards
Though tears ran down my face, for all the lost,
Who once like me had prospect of reward –

That place above purchased at such a cost.
We'd not discussed or mentioned this before 200
In travelling here, but now we reached, at last,

A point at centre, at evil's dead core;
So Dante told me straight: 'Cancer can kill,
But of the grace of God you can be sure;

This truth, believed, helps you escape these ills
Whereby these damned are stuck and come to nothing,
Except to know they caused just what they feel.

We must depart. But wolves in sheep's soft clothing
Exactly states what this realm's all about,
For self-destruction comes from hard self-loathing.' 210

Then Dante paused, his eyes looked up and out,
As if some distant future he saw clear;
Yet one to be had only by this route

We now pursued of obstacles and fear.
His finger pointed to a nearby bed
In which one Rich sat and venomously sneered.

But while he did, sniffling, he scratched his head,
As if perplexed, though how could that be so?
For Rich knew thinking backwards, always led;

How could there be ideas he didn't know? *220*
'Recall,' said Dante, 'your friend Ginty's boasts?'
Yes, (though I'd hoped that was where we'd not go) -

'Well, Oxford, England proves a fertile host
To entertain and spread mental pandemics
That waste the land and leave the people lost.

This Rich seems harmless, a mere academic,
Armchair critic, as it were, and see –
The pure beneficence his actions mimic:

Fair-minded helper of humanity,
What does science say, where's the evidence? *230*
All nice, concealing vicious, vile envy;

Determination, ruthless, to advance
His own career, get others too to laugh
At God, and make-believe that that's real science.

So here he is, examining his own stuff
And what it means, which he can't piece together:
Not nous to own he doesn't know enough;

That what he is, and what He is, grows ever
Wider - a gulf no thinking bridges, spans,
And ignorance never excuses either. *240*

The certainties on which he took his stand
Unravel, as Penelope's weaving did,
Which meant no suitor heard the wedding banns,

Attended marriage, possessed the bride;
But rather all their works remained undone
As Nemesis strode boldly in instead.'

Nemesis! - daughter worse than any son -
Whom Satan's self cannot escape or thwart,
Who binds the giants, holds the Titans down;

No magic works, and no demonic art $_{250}$
Is proof against her power. As the dead mount,
And hell grows rich in all its swelling parts,

Still Satan fears how she could stop his count -
How deepest law, founded in blackest night
Before creation even took its punt,

Before some Fool thought - said - 'Let there be light!',
She, the inexorable, held whole sway,
Destroying - for what, an itch? - wrong and right.

Like superstitious atheists who pray,
So Satan now, incarnate in his Rich, $_{260}$
Aware that wealth could all be lost someday

If omens took a nasty turn or pitch,
So how provide some guarantee for sure?
He reaches down and smooths his bulging crotch -

Out comes his worm the Babylonian whore
Adored in AD Sixty-Six, and now:
Elongating, snake-headed, one-eyed, dire -

Such heralded all his powers on huge show.
Its markings, slick, severe, attractive yet
Finally sickening as it grew and grew. $_{270}$

But as he stroked it, as one would a pet,
Revelling in strength stoked between his thighs,
Distilling what's spiritual till it felt wet,

From which sour source - drawing to it black flies -
Nib-like, his penis wrote the cosmic contract:
One third part his for all eternities.

Damn Nemesis, Chaos, or other acts!
There! Rich held his pen - and no matter what
Happened in future, Satan had his pact.

Certain. But Rich then flinched, some tremor shot $_{280}$
Through him, and his hand paused from his writing;
As if in getting, something was not got:

Mere scrawling wreckage, from his head's dull striking
And gouging marks on a lax putty plaque
On which no character formed, but sheer blank blighting.

How now he wished, perhaps, he could go back,
Unsay the wonderment he once expressed,
Transfixed with powers he thought his own mind packed -

Missing the memes from ancient times no less
That spoke so clearly of a One - a Day - $_{290}$
When every eye would witness true prowess,

When gibbering tongues in full babble would stay
Their motion – when all the trembling world stopped
And held its breath in fear: what would One say?

'I say no evidence; fairies are rot;
If there is God – primitive idea – God's
Evil – the wars men have pointlessly fought;

And how can there be evil if God's good?'
Some energy of old flushed, flooding in,
If not changing truth, then altering mood; $_{300}$

But even as he revved his ranting spin
A slither of light caught his cardigan
Ever so slightly, dissolving it skein,

So that beneath, his skin - of thinnest dun -
Surfaced in dissolute, dissolving form;
But I gasped – for light – seemed like from the sun.

But how - in this depth! - below living worms?
A ward where no windows were, and no gaps,
Far, far beyond substance and time's taut terms,

113

How could sunshine be, how explain this lapse? *310*
His face now creased with horror at the touch -
Rays potent as through magnifying glass;

Or like some kettle boiling steam too much,
So skin began to hiss, flake off in clouds
Of drear smoke, acrid as acid's sharp scorch.

Amazed I looked, and Dante cried aloud –
Was that in pain or in an ecstasy?
I saw him shield his eyes, hand on his brow.

'Lo! Lo! See! See!' And then it dawned on me:
Like being at a beach at morning-tide *320*
And up the sun comes irresistibly

Dazzling, waves reflecting good's true side,
So that we see and through our seeing, know;
Though who could stare direct, yet we both tried?

Before us the god of the golden bow
Appeared, as effortless as a light beam,
And Dante bowed his head, 'My lord Apollo.'

About his being flickered photon-streams
In constant interplay with the black air
Which - forced back - radiance overcame; *330*

For his presence meant it could not be there.
Rich, then, in all this light looked horrified –
His skin and bone all set to disappear

Into the big nothing in which he'd died;
But now one last throw of dice he threw out:
He croaked in throaty chokes, 'This won't abide –

This isn't real – real science demands doubt –
This trickery won't do – I'm...' his voice trailed
Off. Done, compelled through light to total rout.

Confront Apollo? Dared! And now he'd failed; *340*
The sludge of what he was dripped pointlessly
Away, along with words that mocked and railed.

But as he melted, so too some deep freeze
Contracted him at core - Apollo's beams
No longer touched his essence, or his sleaze;

Shuddering within, his presence all condemned,
As absence now began to eat his lies -
Soul stacked in ice as by fire he's consumed.

But I could not withdraw my eager eyes -
Though staring hurt so hard - from seeing him: *350*
The young god of the sun without disguise,

Who shone immortal - shone from every limb -
Each one a perfect form suffused with youth,
Aglow with health untouched by this sick slime;

The while – behold! - prophetic eyes held truth
Whose viewing found me powerless to stand,
For who can endure reality's pith?

What did I see – my future, he unwound
Before my very soul? I gasped again
And as I did so, toppled to the ground. *360*

But Dante's arm caught me and took the strain:
So I, suspended, tilted in mid-air,
As one rushing, desperate for his name.

How long I do not know, but sounds of prayer
Surged forward from within my deepest part,
But what I thought inside now pounded clear

As thunder, lightning stir in truest hearts,
Foreshadowing rain's new life that is to be.
'Apollo!' my heart cried, 'teach me your art:

I always honoured you - my destiny! ₃₇₀
Inspire me now with that full Orphic load
You gave your son in hell to now give me.'

And as my prayer completed, a road,
Subtle, unseen, which I'd not known before
Became apparent, and only just ahead.

Apollo seemed not to move, but I swear
His head turned - on his face some slight smile,
As if encouragement, to bless me here.

Dante, impatient, urged me on the while.
'We cannot stay – Apollo's shown the way: ₃₈₀
Through him you quit this morass, find your style,

As once long ago I too was raised.'
Beneath my feet some tremor pulsed its quake,
Portending Sodom and its end of days.

Tempted, I forced myself to not look back;
I knew the penalty that would incur –
Orpheus suffered as he turned on his track

And doubted Death's word he'd release his soul; her
Whose beauty outweighed the whole universe,
Straying behind him, never to be there ₃₉₀

When light struck flesh emerging from hell's curse:
His own soul fading, lost amidst the wraiths,
And no song strong enough – what could be worse?

But Phoebus had smiled - urging I had faith;
Beside me too immortal Dante lived;
I fixed my full will on the living path,

Wrenching my being from all that's depraved,
The vileness of myself seen in these wards,
Praying as I did so, I could be saved -

That mighty Phoebus and one greater Lord 400
Might hear my plea and in this desperate strait –
O God! – I might come to where I am purged.

The ground lurched - gave way - for time would not wait;
These wards were due to sink down in their lakes
Of fire, and I must leap to miss their fates.

I heard behind chaos, like timber, crack;
And then perpetual ruin, as if mad,
Asylum-bound souls screeched for their own wrack.

But I, on a solid stairwell, now stood,
Weeping. Who could not, at such loss of good? 410

ACKNOWLEDGEMENTS

Thanks to the following publications in which my work has appeared, and to some heroes who have supported me:

UK
> Dawntreader
> Bournemouth Library
> Towards Wholeness
> Storgy
> Quaker News and Views

USA
> The Society of Classical Poets
> Anglo Theological Review
> Ancient Paths Literary Magazine
> The Epoch Times
> The Lowestoft Chronicle
> Midwest Book Review

Evan Mantyk, Nicolas Litchfield, Carol Smallwood, Sharon Kilarski, Josh and Channaly Phillip, Ross Jeffrey, Roz Smith, Simon J Harris

ABOUT THE AUTHOR

James Sale has been a writer for over 50 years, and has had over 40 books published, including 9 collections of poetry, as well as books from Macmillan/Nelson (The Poetry Show volumes 1, 2, 3), Pearson (York Notes: Macbeth, Six Women Poets), and other major publishers (Hodder & Stoughton, Longmans, Folens, Stanley Thornes) on how to teach the writing of poetry. Most recently his poems have appeared in the UK in many magazines. He won 2nd Prize in The Society of Classical Poets (New York) 2014 Annual Poetry Competition and First prize in their 2017 competition and was invited to join their Advisory Board. He has had over 400 blogs published, many on literary themes and reviews, online as well as in magazines. He is also a commissioned feature writer on culture for New York's Epoch Times. James was a co-founder and director of the KQBX Press, which published dozens of poets before it closed in the late 90s, including: Sean Street, Michael Henry, Brian Hinton, Sarah Hopkins, and Helen Flint. Finally, the Bournemouth Yellow Buses company selected James as one of their top six poets as part of their marketing campaign around the town in 2016. He was given a free bus pass as part of the deal – nice!

INTERVIEW WITH JAMES SALE

Q1. Poetry has always been with humankind, yet these days it seems to get a bad rap. As a modern-day poet, why do you think poetry is still important and what do you think we can learn from it?

We can learn everything from it. Apollo, the god of poetry was also the god healing, and healing and poetry are intimately connected. Narrative is a primary act of mind, and poetry is a special form of it which restores balance since it draws on both forms of knowing – both right (creative) and left (rational) sides of the brain. In this way it reveals what we did not know before – anyone who thinks that one can write poetry by willing it, knows nothing about the process. It is a profound form of therapy that starts with the individual – and may remain there – but in good or even great poetry the therapy spreads out to the whole community as they begin to heal. For what does the poetry do? It gives a language in which our current psychoses can be expressed and even understood. That starts the healing process.

Q2. *The English Cantos* is your attempt to write an epic in the style of Dante Alighieri. Could you please give us some background on why you chose Dante, rather than, let's say,

Homer, as your model, and what this means for your poetry?

This is a difficult question to answer without sounding pretentious. I am not pretending to be Homer or Dante, or to be as good a poet as they were. But the thing is: the greats of the past provide us with models for today. The models may be thematic or they can be formal. Homer's model of verse in hexameters is too remote for me to use today. But Italian has long provided the English language with fabulous forms that we can adapt and use; most famously, of course, the sonnet, which since its importation some 500 years ago has produced some of our greatest poetry. But the English language seems to have an aversion to odd-numbered structures. Paul Fussell observed, 'The failure of terza rima to establish a tradition in English, as well as the general rarity of successful English three-line stanzas, suggests that stanzas of even- rather than odd-numbered lines are those that appeal most naturally to the Anglo-Saxon sensibility.' However, when I examined this matter, I found – for example, in Shelley's The Triumph of Life – that the joy of terza rima was its ability to have the concentration of a sonnet (through its rhyme scheme) and yet to have a propulsive narrative power. This is seen most clearly in Dante. Of course, the key thing is not to set oneself the misguided task of insisting on perfect rhymes, since our language is not as rich in them as Italian. The significance of this for today's poetry is that it provides an avenue in which to explore real poetry that requires artistry, and to break the tyranny of low expectations which constitutes free verse.

Q3. *The English Cantos* is not only a homage to Dante, however, but also a deeply personal work, in that it explores your own battle with cancer via the metaphor of a journey through hell; the story is even set in a hospital ward. How does your real-life experience, and the concept of hell, connect?

As you know, I was in hospital for 3 months and nearly died; I came to a point – having lost nearly 5 stone in weight – of feeling almost vaporised. And in the midst of all this - people around me dying - I had a Near-Death Experience. Somebody once said that religion is for those afraid to go to hell, and spirituality is for those who have been there! And it's said too, that the great archetypal poet, Orpheus, made his own hell in choosing to descend there to rescue his own lost soul; but if he could create it, then he could also prevail against it. So I think in some way, without even knowing it, I was lost and had lost my way, and so I had to undertake this journey. Indeed, by the grace of God, I was spared to make it. William Blake wrote: 'Go to heaven for form and to hell for energy, and marry the two'. There is a wild energy in hell, but under heaven this can take form and become a thing of great beauty. Such is my desire.

Q4. One of the really startling things about *The English Cantos* is the narrative drive. How difficult was it to create this sense of pace and were there any major obstacles you encountered during the writing process that you had to overcome?

The biggest problem is always the same: what next? You start with an idea and then the Muse gets to work – if you invoke the Muse – and then, where to? To write the poetry is to enter the trance state where the visions start forming, but for this to become poetry the other side of the brain has to simultaneously function by providing a form of words that mimetically enact the energy of the vision. I absolutely believe that in some profound sense I am not writing the poem – except maybe the worst bits – but some power is writing through me, and this power is solving the problem of what next. But there are two problems with this: the first, is the fear that one will be abandoned by the Muse, for one is not in control of Her. And second, while Her power is infinite, the instrument She takes possession of is limited – imagine, She is the volcano about to blow red-hot and vital lava, and you are a plastic straw through which She must be funnelled? Block-age, or what? The work of the poet's lifetime is to prepare him or herself so that their 'vehicle' is larger, better, more able to accommodate the full offering of the Muse. I believe that the great prophets of the Old Testament were in a similar position. Poets in one sense, of course, are prophets.

Q5. Dante, along with various other historical, mythologi-cal, and even contemporary personages appear in *The English Cantos*. How did you go about re-creating these characters, and to what extent do you expect people to find some of the more hidden references and meanings in the poem?

Unlike James Joyce, I am not seeking to create a work that keeps academics in business for 400 years working out every nuance and allusion. Goethe said that 'Personality is everything in art and poetry', so all great works will be imbued by personality, which inevitably means the personal as well as the general. Dante's poem is massively structured along the lines of Catholic theology, and I feel it would be tedious to repeat that. Instead, what I have done is sought after a more personal interpretation of what hell, purgatory and heaven might mean in the contemporary world. Since this world is no longer theistic in terms of its culture, it is useless to cite dogmatics at it; on the contrary, one needs to use subjective and psychological experience in order to flesh out what this means. To this end, then, the poem does various things in reverse to what Dante might have done. For example, like Dante the first Canto is not in hell proper, but being in the hospital ward dying of cancer becomes the gateway through which I then enter hell. So my first real experience actually in hell is Canto 2. This is where I meet my dead mother. In Dante (who never, incidentally meets his mother in hell!) the lesser sins are in the opening cantos, since the sins are all hierarchically aligned; but in my vision, perhaps the worst thing of all is meeting my own mother - certainly psychologically the affect of the mother on the child is almost certainly the most beneficial or the most devastating. Effectively, then, I go straight in at the deep end, because this is what it means to me. I then pursue this thread with a range of people I have known whom we can all identify with: for example, one's boss, and especially one's friend, and of these I consider 3 false friends covering most of my lifetime. But as we explore different wards in this hospital we encounter the bigger, more generic issues of our times: the Iraq War, Brexit, the fame of false poets, the false philosophers who have led the people astray. Though I may not know some of these people personally, unlike earlier on, I find that the Muse is able to write about them - I hope convincingly - because I am not focusing on information, data or stats: I focus on just why they infuriate and anger me with their deceptions. Hence, I believe, why the poem has so much energy and forward momentum. You will not need to identify hidden references in the poem to enjoy; but there will be some joys there for those who like these things!

Q6. Which was your favourite scene of the *Cantos* to write? Can you tell us why?

This is an extraordinarily difficult question to answer, and I am not sure I can. As egotistical as it sounds, I actually like all the Cantos and loved writing them all. I guess there comes a special satisfaction – at least for me – when the situation suddenly takes a dramatic turn AND at that point some supernal or supernatural or mythological agency intervenes. I love those moments, and as I am writing the end of Canto 12 as I now write this, I am hoping to produce such a climax in the last to match the others. But a good example of what I mean occurred in the extract of Canto 9 that appeared on The Society of Classical Poets' website: https://bit.ly/ 2W4Rwut. So, having escaped from the ward of my next door neighbour who literally was a murderer of his wife, I am reflecting on his self-destruction and conclude:

For each one, yes, against their own soul sins,
    As Dathan, Korah and Abiram found,
    Like scorpions perishing from their own stings;
    Only unlike such piercings was the ground
    As Moses summoned the people stand back,
    And all the earth where Korah was, and sand
    Around his tents shifted to void and slack
    And down they went, still living ... for a while ...
    Till covered and lost in a soundless black.

In writing this I was very excited by the aptness of the Dathan ... Moses references, which I think gave it a sombre finality.

Q7. You have been writing poetry for some fifty years or more, and have had numerous books on how to write and study poetry published, including *The Poetry Show* and the best-selling *York Notes: Macbeth*. What other poetical influences are there on your writing and what other poets do you recommend readers explore?

Probably the three greatest English speaking poetic influences on my work are Milton, GM Hopkins and WB Yeats, and what they have in common, of course, is form – a severe and relentless sense of form, but one that takes risks with the rules. Indeed, bends them to their purpose of deeper levels of meaning, often polysemic. Furthermore, they are experts in the deployment of iambic verse, which is the means in English for all our deepest utter-

ances. At different points in my life I have tried to write like each of them. So I love this and them. People deceive themselves if they think 'free verse' can get anywhere near the power and potential of iambic verse; but it is a delusion that most people want to embrace because the word 'free' gives it a right-on political dimension that is entirely misplaced in this context. What I recommend, therefore, is - if you want to write real poetry - study any of the writers who seriously use form, and in particular deploy iambic verse regularly in their verse. To be clear here: there are some good 'free verse' poems, but not many, and most of it is just chopped-up prose.

Q8. In Italian Catholicism there is a concept of "*contra-passo*" where the punishment fits the crime. You seem to rigorously adhere to this in *The English Cantos*, which gives your hell a psychological dimension, much like Dante's. How did exploring *contrapasso* influence your work on the *Cantos*? Did it throw up any revelations?

I am glad you mention this. It is difficult meeting people in various states of punishment and finding different ways to punish them! At the end of the day, we are all going to reap what we sow. But I think there are some revelations along the way. An unexpected one occurred in the Canto 12 I am currently writing: in Canto 6 I am attacked by my friend and it really hurts because I believe he is powerful and 'real', but in Canto 12 my mentor, Dante, is attacked viciously by one of the false philosophers, but – I realised – the blow had to have no effect because the philosophy itself was 'unreal' – and Dante knew that. I think the reader will find lots of unexpected incidents that on reflection 'suit' the crime. I surely hope so.

Q9. Like Dante's epic, *The English Cantos* will explore Hell, but also Purgatory and Heaven. How do you plan to tackle Purgatory and Heaven, which may have a very different cosmology and tone to that of Hell?

I intend to be very specific here and follow my own medical experience of being in the hospital. First, in hell, I was confined to the bed and the wards I was in. But as I started recovering, I was able to step out and travel a little – down to where they had a small chapel, St Luke's – remember, the physician evangelist! – where one could pray and meditate; which I did many times. So purgatory will begin as I ascend the stairs from the wards to the chapel. Then, once I got even better still, I was allowed out – and my wife Linda conducted me – to visit the small duck pond in the hospital grounds. To be there in the sunshine, recovering my life, was a kind of heaven all itself. So these are the structural points, and I think they will involve a different kind of cosmology. I certainly think for the first canto in purgatory I have an astonishing opening gambit that would have amazed Dante, and yet I think I have based it on his ideas too! Naturally, the tone will change. Each section has to have its own feel. The sharpness of the language in hell must ultimately give way to a more liquid, flowing style where light is everything.

Thank you for this interview. Your questions have been very insightful. I'd probably conclude by saying that, regarding the HellWard section of The English Cantos, the concept of hell is unpopular to the exact degree that freedom of the will is unpopular - today we all want to be victims. In this important way the poem follows Dante, since freedom of the will was the central premise on which his poem was built. As Dorothy Sayers says it: 'Hell is the enjoyment of your own way forever'. In other words, it's not so much that God puts us there, but that we end up where we want to be. Some people love their misery.

CONTRIBUTORS TO THE WIDER CIRCLE

Joseph Sale – Novelist, Writer, & Editor, Linda E. Sale – Artist, Robert Monaghan – Film Director & Game Designer, Evan Mantyk – President of the Society of Classical Poets, Pat Yates – Quaker, friend, and poetry enthusiast, J. Simon Harris – Poet & Translator, James B. Nicola – Poet, Steve Feltham – www.choralifiscus.org, Pascoe Sawyers – DJ & Author, J. D. Wallace – Professor of Communication Studies, Theresa Rodriguez – author of *Jesus and Eros: Sonnets, Poems and Songs*, David Orme – retired children's writer and religious art enthusiast, Angela Perrett – Artist, Judith Warbey — Artist, David B. Gosselin – a student of classics and languages based in Montreal, T. M. Moore – poet and Principle of The Fellowship of Ailbe, Brian Jenner – Speechwriter, Author & Event Organiser, & Sue Kerr – Art collector.

Printed in Great Britain
by Amazon